Praise for
A Not-So-Simple Life

"As Maya Stark pours her heart out in her journal, readers are treated to an inside view of a life that is at times exotic and unfamiliar and at other times hauntingly similar to our own. Maya's struggles become our struggles, her pain our pain, and her successes, therefore, even sweeter. *A Not-So-Simple Life* is another triumph for Melody Carlson."

> —VIRGINIA SMITH, author of *Sincerely, Mayla* and *Stuck in the Middle*

"Fantastic book! Maya is so easy to like—this is a hard story to put down!"

> —ERYNN MANGUM, author of *Miss Match*

"Melody Carlson has proven her skill once again at writing gritty stories about characters in difficult situations. In *A Not-So-Simple Life,* Maya Stark seeks to escape life under the controlling hand of her drug-addicted mother by acting on a plan for independence with admirable determination."

> —MICHELLE BUCKMAN, author of *Maggie Come Lately* and *My Beautiful Disaster*

"I just finished Melody's book and loved it! The journal format makes the story, and Maya, so real and believable. Readers will easily be able to identify with the realistic approach to a prevalent situation."

> —PATRICIA RUSHFORD, author of the Max & Me Mysteries

Books by Melody Carlson:

Piercing Proverbs

DIARY OF A TEENAGE GIRL SERIES

<u>Caitlin O'Conner:</u>

Becoming Me

It's My Life

Who I Am

On My Own

I Do!

<u>Chloe Miller:</u>

My Name Is Chloe

Sold Out

Road Trip

Face the Music

<u>Kim Peterson:</u>

Just Ask

Meant to Be

Falling Up

That Was Then…

THE SECRET LIFE OF SAMANTHA MCGREGOR SERIES

Bad Connection

Beyond Reach

Playing with Fire

Payback

NOTES FROM A SPINNING PLANET SERIES

Ireland

Papua New Guinea

Mexico

TRUE COLORS SERIES

A
Not-So-
Simple
Life

Diary of a Teenage Girl

Maya Book Nº. 1

A Not-So-Simple Life

a novel

MELODY CARLSON

MULTNOMAH
BOOKS

A NOT-SO-SIMPLE LIFE
PUBLISHED BY MULTNOMAH BOOKS
12265 Oracle Boulevard, Suite 200
Colorado Springs, Colorado 80921

ISBN: 978-1-60142-117-3

Published in the United States by WaterBrook Multnomah, an imprint of the
Crown Publishing Group, a division of Random House Inc., New York.

MULTNOMAH and its mountain colophon are registered trademarks of Random
House Inc.

Library of Congress Cataloging-in-Publication Data
Carlson, Melody.
    A not-so-simple life : a novel / Melody Carlson.
        p. cm. — (Diary of a teenage girl. Maya ; bk. 1)
    Summary: Maya keeps a journal the year following her aunt's death, in which
she records her thoughts about her alcoholic and drug-addicted mother and her
own feelings of depression, until she decides to give her heart to God.
    ISBN 978-1-60142-117-3
    1. Cousins—Fiction. 2. Family problems—Fiction. 3. Emotional problems—
Fiction. 4. Christian life—Fiction. 5. Diaries—Fiction. I. Title.
    PZ7.C216637 2008
    [Fic]—dc22

                                           2008008033

Printed in the United States of America
2010

10 9 8 7 6 5 4 3

One

May 10

These two things I know for sure: (1) nothing about life is fair, and (2) it is not going to get better. How's that for an optimistic way to begin this journal? Not that I'll continue this exercise in depressing futility. I mean, how can writing about my miserable life improve one single part of it? The only reason I'm even attempting this now is my cousin Kim Peterson. A cousin I didn't even know existed just a couple of weeks ago. Not that she's actually related. Not genetically anyway. Kim's mother, who died before I could even meet her, was my mom's sister. I suppose if I'd known her, I might've called her "Aunt Patricia." Or not. But Kim, since she was adopted from Korea, is *not* an actual relative. Although I suppose that I sort of wish she were...but that's my secret.

Anyway, as if I needed help to confirm my theory (that life is not fair), by the time I learned about this mystery aunt, she was already dying from cancer. My "cousin" Kim (who I think is seventeen—anyway she's a couple of years older than me) had done an extensive online search to dredge up Shannon (that's my mom). Kim's plan had been to reconnect the two sisters. They'd been out of contact for more than thirty years, and Patricia was longing to see her younger sister before it was too late.

As fate would have it, that happy little family reunion never took place. And naturally, I blame Shannon for this unfortunate fact. Although she knew her sister was terminally ill, instead of booking the next plane out there, she went shopping. Shannon, being Shannon, set out for the swankiest shops in Beverly Hills in search of the "perfect" outfit—something she planned to wear in order to "impress" her dying sister. As it turned out, she wore that stupid outfit to Patricia's funeral.

My aunt's funeral still feels rather surreal to me—like I wasn't actually there, or perhaps I was simply watching a movie about some nice family who had lost a loved one. And as I sat there in the front row with my mom and Kim and her dad, listening to the preacher going on and on about how wonderful this Patricia person was and how everyone who knew her loved her, all I could think was how totally unfair it was that I'd never known her. And how I never even got a chance to meet her. Never said hello or good-bye. Nothing.

Because it occurred to me, sitting there and staring at a small sea of flowers, that I would've liked this woman. She sounded kind and thoughtful and truly good. Good in a way that you just don't see down here in L.A. And although I don't consider myself to be "good" in that sense, I do think that in some small way I might be a little bit like my aunt. But now I'll never really find out.

Of course I blame Shannon for that too. And rightly so. For starters, she never even told me that I had an aunt. And then when Kim contacted her, Shannon acted as if she'd been the one cast aside by her older sister. Come to find out, it was Shannon who had run away, leaving her home and family far behind, and then never getting back in touch with any of them. It's hard to admit this, especially here in Beverly Hills, where they're a dime a dozen, but my mom is a real phony.

"Patricia is dying," she had sobbed to me after the phone call a couple of weeks ago.

"Who's Patricia?" I thought it was probably one of her drug friends, perhaps someone who'd OD'd or gotten in a car wreck while driving under the influence. These things do happen...I know.

"*My sister!*" Shannon cried out, acting like I should've known this already, like it was an established fact.

"What sister?"

"Patricia Peterson—she's my older sister. That was her daughter on the phone. Patricia is dying, Maya! My *only* sister is dying!"

Then instead of hopping on a plane like a normal person who had just learned her long-lost sister was dying,

Shannon insisted on taking me shopping for most of the following day. She claimed I needed something "decent" to wear for the trip. Of course, this was totally bogus, but feeling sorry for her, I played along. So it wasn't until later that evening that Shannon finally did a quick online search for cheap airline tickets. She wanted to get a deal on airfare—and that same day she'd just paid more than twelve hundred dollars for a Dolce & Gabbana purse!

So it seems that stupid designer bag, which not only looks almost exactly like another purse in Shannon's cluttered closet but is also made of real leather (suggesting that an innocent cow gave up its life so my mom could spend way too much money on a purse that she didn't even need), was the main reason we missed the opportunity to see her sister while she was still alive. Okay, it sounds like I'm blaming the purse. As usual, the only one to blame here is Shannon.

Perhaps now you see how my theory about life *not* getting any better proves itself once again. And Kim wants me to write about all this in a stupid diary! Like she thinks it's going to be cathartic and revealing and "spiritual" (that's what she told me). But instead, I'm feeling more bummed than ever. Recording the sad bits and pieces of my life in a journal feels like one great big downer. And yet, I think it's for Kim's sake I am still writing.

I don't know why I even care about her. Furthermore, I know I made the worst possible impression on both her and her dad. Normally, I wouldn't give a rat's rear end about what other people think of me…but something about those two took me by surprise. Just sitting with them at my aunt's funeral, observing their faces, their sadness, or the way they interacted with all their friends—their many, many friends. Well, as much as I don't want to, *I do care.* And that bugs me. But the fact is, I like them. I like them both. Not that they would have the slightest clue of this. No, there's not a chance they would suspect as much. Because I'm absolutely, positively certain that they both think I am (1) a totally spoiled brat, (2) a moody, self-centered adolescent, and (3) just plain rude.

Oh, did I mention that my mom and I got into a huge ugly argument right after we met Kim and my uncle? Uncle Allen was driving us home from the airport, and he and Kim were being rather quiet—probably still dealing with their own shock and grief. Patricia had been dead for less than twenty-four hours at the time. And admittedly, her death had taken my mom and me by surprise as well. Not that it gave us an excuse to act like morons. So when Shannon made some stupid comment that suggested she was the only one hurting over Patricia's death, well, that just got to me.

And Shannon and I got into the worst catfight ever— including a colorful exchange of some foul words I'm sure neither Kim nor her dad has ever used. Not one of my proudest moments. And yet, I just couldn't stop myself. That's how much my mom gets to me. Sometimes I hate her so deeply that I think I could kill her while she's passed out on the sofa. Then sometimes I feel so brokenhearted sorry for her, and I realize that I'm the only one she has, and I am torn in two—split right down the middle.

Take today...or what actually began yesterday morning when Shannon was in one of her moods. She was stomping around the house, acting like she was the only one in the world who had ever suffered.

"Your father is late again!" she snapped at me, like it was my personal fault that my dad's monthly alimony and child-support payment hadn't arrived yet. I mean, at least the guy pays.

"So..." I just shrugged and started to make coffee.

"So?" Now Shannon was in my face. Without any makeup, her normally angular face looked puffy and blotchy, the telltale signs of a late-night drinking binge. And just a couple of days ago she told me she had quit. Again. "So, that means we're out of money, Maya. Out of money."

I shrugged again. Nothing new about that either. Still, I kept my thoughts to myself. I know my mom's moods well enough to know when to hold my tongue. First her mood swings, and next it's her fist.

"Well, in case you've forgotten, no money means no food."

I opened the fridge to see that, as usual, it was fairly empty. A couple of microbrew beers, some Dijon, a jar of olives, a hard wedge of cheese, and several bottles of Evian. Fortunately, I'd been learning to garden this year. And being a vegan, I usually subsisted by what Shannon called "grazing" out in the backyard. I was growing several things, including tomatoes, cucumbers, lettuce, green onions, and the start of some good-looking white corn. It was better than going hungry.

I'm sure this would seem ironic to some people, since we live in a house worth at least three million. Or it was worth that much before Shannon mortgaged it several times. Who knows what it's worth now? Or who owns it? The bank or my mom?

"He'll pay." I poured coffee beans into the grinder. "He always does...eventually." Then I turned on the small appliance, allowing the loud noise to block out Shannon's response to my nonchalance. It worked. Because by the time I finished, she was gone. But she was still fuming. And before long she left the house without saying where she was going or when she would be back. That's when I knew it was going to get worse.

But having learned the art of denial from the queen herself, I pretended nothing was wrong. As usual, I got on my computer and began doing schoolwork. Oh, yeah, did I mention that I'm "homeschooled"? Or at least that's what we call it. The truth is, I school myself. After I got into trouble in middle school and after Shannon came down to the school and made the trouble much, much worse, it was decided that I would be homeschooled.

I didn't complain about this decision. At the time, it sounded like a nice escape. It wasn't until a few months had gone by that I realized what I'd given up. But by then I was worried that I couldn't get it back. Even if I could slip back into classes—and I've always been smart—I just wasn't sure if I could slip back into my friends. I guess you could say I'd burned a few bridges. And so (perhaps this shows what a coward I really am beneath my bravado) I continued on with this farce of an education. But by the time my peers were entering high school, I decided that I didn't want to grow up to be a total idiot, so I forced my mom to order some real curriculum, which I access via my laptop. And I suppose that, for the most part, I am keeping up. But really, who knows? Who cares?

I do know that I envied Kim and her friends from school while we were there. I watched her classmates interacting with her after her mom's funeral. I saw the way they hugged her and spoke to her and seemed to genuinely care about her. And I tried not to notice how many stopped by her house in the following days. All expressing love and grief and what seemed like sincere friendship. And as I pretended not to witness these irksome things, I was fully aware that I was missing out on something important. Even now I feel like I've been robbed or cheated, or maybe I'm just stuck.

But back to Shannon and how she was AWOL all day and all night yesterday. And as they say, the writing was on the wall. It started with her drinking binge, followed by the fact that she was obviously out getting high. She'd probably called Luis (one of her favorite drug buddies) and told him her sob story about losing her only sister to cancer. I'm sure that must've been worth a pretty good hit of something. And when she finally came home this afternoon, she was totally wasted. I'm not even sure how she could drive, but her car seemed to be intact. Now she is sleeping it off—or else she's dead—but she hasn't moved for hours from her position on the living room sofa. And now it's evening, and I am back in the attic. This is where I usually end up after she falls off the wagon.

Don't get me wrong. It's not as if my mom sends me up here as some sort of punishment for her stupidity. No, that might be considered abuse or neglect or just plain parental meanness. No, retreating to the attic has been my own little escape plan over the years. I feel safer up here, and so far she has yet to figure it out. I have an old denim futon and a lava lamp and a few other comforts. And if I open both windows, the cooler air eventually flows through. Really, it's not so bad. And it's quiet. Although there are times when my little hideaway feels more like a prison cell than a private retreat. And sometimes, like tonight, I wonder why I do this to myself. Even more than that, I wonder…will this ever end?

Speaking of ends, I hate to end my first entry in my first journal on such a depressing note. Therefore I'll take a small detour now. Perhaps I can even consider this part of my homeschooling. Like anyone is paying attention. Just the same, I've secretly dreamed of having my own "green" column. Or perhaps my own "green" blog. Hey, I may not be Ed Begley Jr., but I can do my small part to save the planet. So I will practice these earth-friendly tidbits right here in my journal. And who knows…maybe someday they will be read by others. Anyway, here goes my first attempt.

Maya's Green Tip for the Day

Did you know that we consume nearly <u>thirty billion</u> bottles of water in the United States every year? That's mountains of plastic water bottles that have been used once, then tossed out. My state actually recycles water bottles but only when we collect them and turn them in. Here's what I do. I have several reusable water bottles that can go through the dishwasher. And I've found that water from the tap isn't much different than what can be purchased, so I keep a refillable water filter pitcher in the fridge. I use that to fill my water bottle with cool, clean water and—presto—I'm ready to roll.

Two

May 11

Shannon is very sorry first thing this morning. I am surprised to find her up so early, sitting outside drinking coffee like it is just another day. Except she has a whopper of a headache and some really bad jitters—like she's coming down from her chemical high. And naturally, this makes her somewhat grouchy and unpredictable. It's like she's suffering from a multiple personality disorder. Sort of a Dr. Jekyll and Ms. Hyde kind of thing. One minute she's sorry; the next minute she's biting my head off. Talk about walking on eggshells.

So I do what I've always done. A little something I learned to do after Dad left, back when I was seven and desperately trying to hold things together. I become the caregiver, and I attempt to placate my mother—her wish becomes my command. And not surprisingly, she's hungry now. This is always the case after a binge of something like cocaine or another kind of upper that temporarily replaces the appetite with a false sense of energy. I've seen it before. I'll probably see it again.

And our refrigerator is bare. So I ride my bike to the closest store and, using my own money, get a few very expensive groceries. Then I come home and fix Shannon a late breakfast. Not vegan like I would prepare for myself. But I do make sure it's low cal, low fat, low carb, and high fiber, just the way she likes it. This turns out to be plain nonfat yogurt topped with sweet strawberries (from my garden) and unsweetened granola. To this I add a glass of fresh-squeezed grapefruit juice and whole-wheat toast with real butter. Real butter is Shannon's one dietary indulgence. Go figure. Anyway, she seems happy—briefly. So I sit on the patio and listen to her third or fourth apology of the morning.

"I'm so sorry for what I did yesterday." Her hand shakes as she spoons up another bite of yogurt. "I know I promised you I'd never to do that again..." She's careful not to say what "that" is as she looks at me with teary eyes. "But I've been so devastated over Patricia... I know you must understand how a person who's grieving might stumble like this. It won't happen again, baby. I swear to you it won't."

I don't respond to this overly familiar promise. I just lean back in my chair, averting my eyes as I pretend to study the palm trees along the back wall. I think that one in the corner is dying, but I won't mention it. What would be the point? It's not like we can afford to have it taken out—or any other yard work done, for that matter. Most of all, I don't want Shannon to see that I don't believe her promise and am just disgusted with her in general. And I don't want her to question whether I think she really cared about her deceased sister or was simply using someone else's tragedy as a handy excuse to cave to her own selfish cravings. I've heard that in the mind of an addict, "any excuse is a good excuse to use." And I've seen it enough to believe it's true.

"I never told you much about Patricia, did I?" she continues, oblivious to my general skepticism.

I just shake my head.

"Patricia and I were really close growing up. She was very sweet to me." She sighed. "Our parents were a mess, Maya. I mean, our dad, mostly... I've told you about him before, haven't I?"

I nod, but the truth is, she hasn't told me much. Just that he was a self-centered loser and she couldn't get away from him fast enough. Not that this news surprised me much. I mean, the apple doesn't fall far from the tree, right?

"That man was one mean lowlife. He beat on our mother fairly regularly. And sometimes, if she wasn't handy, he beat on us too."

I'm not sure whether to believe this or not. "He beat on *you?*"

She turns and glares at me with angry blue eyes. "Yes! I've told you that before, Maya! Don't you ever listen to me?"

I quickly nod again, looking away. *Do not engage. Do not rock her boat.* "I didn't remember...," I mutter.

"Well, I remember! There are some things you never forget. No matter how hard you try. And I remember a time when I was home alone with the stupid jerk. I was in my room, just minding my own business, and suddenly he bursts in and accuses me of drinking one of his beers." She kind of chuckles now, and I look at her curiously. "It wasn't funny at the time," she says quickly. "But I actually *had* been sneaking his beers. I was about your age at the time, and I was pretty fed up with things at home. Who could blame me for needing a beer or two to escape the madness? Anyway, he had just slapped me when Patricia walks in and asks what's going on. So he yells at her and tells her to stay out of it and that I'd stolen one of his precious brewskies. He was about to smack me again when she steps between us and tells him that she's the one who took his beer. Of course that was a total lie." Shannon pauses as if to contemplate this. "And then I just sat there on the bed and watched as he laid into her."

"Wow, that must've been hard."

"Yes, it was very hard..." She has a faraway look now, and I'm thinking it must've been a lot harder on my aunt, and that Patricia must've been an awfully selfless person to take her sister's beating for her, but hopefully Shannon doesn't suspect this.

"He was a monster." She takes a bite of toast and slowly chews.

"Is that why you left home?" I know the answer to this

obvious question, but maybe it will help her to talk about it, like some kind of therapy. One can only hope.

"After Patricia left me, going off to college, I was stuck with him and Mom. I was constantly caught in the middle of their never-ending fights, and then there were the beatings... But after Mom died...well, I just couldn't take it anymore. I had to get out."

"So...you left after your mom died?" I'm still trying to piece these random facts together. Shannon has never told me how old she was when she left home, but I'm pretty sure she didn't finish high school.

She sits straighter now, smoothing her rather wild-looking hair. Because it's bleached blond, it can look pretty strange if she doesn't take care of it and condition it regularly, which she obviously hasn't been doing. "And I was extremely good looking," she continues, as if talking to herself. "Everyone said so. I knew I could make my looks work for me. And I did. There was a time when I was one of the hottest young things in Hollywood."

Okay, that's a huge stretch, even for her. But maybe she realizes how delusional this is, because her chin trembles slightly, like she's about to cry. As her lower lip droops and she makes a sad little frown, I notice she's in need of some new collagen injections. Another expense we cannot afford.

"I could still put my looks to good use, Maya. That is, if I set my mind to it and perhaps had a bit more work done. Although everyone says I still look fantastic for…for my age."

Naturally she never mentions what her age really is. Although I happen to know she hit the big 5-0 last year. Of course, no one else is aware of this top-secret fact. I mean, *no one*. Not even my dad. I'm not sure if he's as gullible as he seems about this, or if he's not good at math, or if maybe he, like me, just wants to avoid the conflict. But Shannon tries to make people believe she's barely forty. Better yet, thirty-nine—that magical number that never changes.

"So what would you do?" I know I've just stepped onto thin ice. "I mean, to utilize your looks… Would you go back into acting?"

"You doubt me, don't you?" Her eyes grow hot blue now, like piercing flames ready to slice right through me.

"No…" I look away.

"You do! You think just because you're young and…well, somewhat pretty…that you're better than me, don't you? I can read you like a book, Maya. Why don't you just admit it? You think I'm too old."

"I don't, Shannon. Really. I just wondered what kind of role you might be looking to—"

She stands abruptly, dropping her bowl of unfinished yogurt onto the cement patio, where it shatters into shards of blue porcelain splattered with white globs of yogurt and a smattering of red berries that almost look like spots of blood. In a way it's kind of pretty. I think I could paint a picture of it.

"What?" Shannon screeches. "You don't think I could be hired as an actress now? You think I'm too old? Maybe you'd like to see me cast as a doddering grandmother or an elderly aunt or some pathetic old maid." She's glaring at me now. *"Is that what you think?"*

"No, of course—"

She slaps me hard across the face.

Then I turn and run into the house. Still, I can't escape her cruel words trailing me as she reminds me that I am "selfish, unappreciative, worthless, spoiled, ungrateful..." and some other graphic words I don't care to write down in this journal.

My prison cell is hot and stuffy this afternoon. Even with the windows open, the air barely moves up here. I wish I had grabbed my water bottle or some of those strawberries to bring up here with me. Or even a book or my laptop. As it is, I only have this pitiful journal. And the things I want to write on these crisp white pages are not pretty. They are dark and angry and hopeless. What is the point of recording all this? Really, will I ever want to read it again? Will I ever want to relive my life?

But perhaps someone else will want to know the truth about Maya Stark, only daughter of the renowned Nick Stark. I mean, when I'm gone. And on days like today, I toy with the idea of checking out of here (and I mean permanently). It almost sounds like a good plan. Although I might not be ready for that yet. I still have some fight left in me.

And so my plan, for today anyway, is to sneak back downstairs and go outside and get on my bike and just ride. But I'll wait until it quiets down a little. For the last hour or so, Shannon has been stomping about the house like a wild animal, screaming and yelling and slamming doors and throwing things. I can't imagine the mess she must be making. But I can guess who will be cleaning it up later when she finally crashes...or worse. No school today, kiddies.

For no specific reason, my thoughts drift back to my cousin again. Kim's probably in school right now. She's quite the academic. Her dad even said as much. What would it feel like to have a life like hers? Oh sure, her mom died. And that is sad. But up until then, she had what I would call a rather nice life. And not for the first time, I'm thinking that it's not fair. But that just proves my theory that nothing about life is fair. Of course, I'm only referring to my own life. There are others out there whose lives are far more than fair—they're charmed. Perhaps that's why my life is such a mess. Maybe these things need to balance, like yin and yang. And other than Kim losing her mom, I'd say that she's one of the lucky ones. I mean, she had two normal, well-adjusted, kind, intelligent, loving parents to raise her. And she wasn't even their birth child. How does that work? A kid is born in another country, given up for adoption, and lands with a couple like the Petersons. Why couldn't that have been me? I wonder if I'm too old for adoption.

Now this makes me think of my dad. And really, he's not such a bad guy. A little selfish, yes. And a little cowardly when it comes to Shannon. But he's basically a good-hearted person. And I believe that, beneath it all, he actually loves me. He just doesn't know what to do about it—and to be fair, that has more to do with Shannon than anything else. She makes it nearly impossible for him to be involved with me, other than sending money. More than once she's threatened to kill him if he ever gives her the opportunity, which he doesn't.

But all that aside, he's pretty caught up in his recently revived singing career. It's all he thinks about. Even when he e-mails me, which is seldom, he only tells me about how great it is being onstage again. I know it was tough being a has-been all these years. Sure, he'd play an occasional nightclub and a gig here and there in some of the second-rate Las Vegas casino hotels. But as someone who was a big pop star in the eighties and pretty much a nobody in the nineties, he's more than a little excited to be booking real concerts now. Consequently, he's busy. Too busy to be bugged by his gloomy teenage daughter complaining about her miserable little life. Although I suppose I could e-mail him and remind him to send money. At least that might make Shannon happy.

For some reason I think of my cousin again, remembering the time Kim asked me, "Why do you call your mom 'Shannon'?"

I think I sort of shrugged and probably rolled my eyes, like, *Why not?* But she wasn't satisfied with that response.

"Don't you *ever* call her Mom?" she persisted.

"Not since my dad left."

"When was that?"

I explained that I'd been around seven and that there'd been a big fight and that Shannon had been the instigator and that she'd probably been high or drunk or something. "So you couldn't really blame him for leaving. She might've killed him."

"Wow, that must've been rough."

"Pretty much." I pretended to be mesmerized by an article about recycling during this conversation. Playing my familiar role of "earth girl," I was reading some green magazine that I'd picked up at the mall.

"Do you see him very often?"

I set my magazine down and gave Kim my best impatient look. "He's busy." I spoke to her like I was explaining something to a five-year-old. "His career is taking off again, and he has his hands full right now." Well, that pretty much shut her up, at least for the time being. It wasn't very nice, but it was the best I could do, considering that I wanted to tear into her. I wanted to yell and cry and carry on like a toddler, pointing out that not all parents are like her parents and that maybe she should just keep her mouth shut about me and my mixed-up family, thank you very much! But at least I knew better. I was, after all, a guest in their home.

Speaking of their home, it was like something out of an old family sitcom. I mean, the rooms screamed "middle-class America" like nothing I'd ever seen before in real life. At first I wanted to make fun of it, but then I actually started to like it. The frumpy and slightly worn furniture started to feel homey and rather comforting—kind of like a pair of broken-in Earth Shoes or a much-laundered pair of well-worn jeans. Shannon thought it was a silly little house—and she even said as much in front of Kim and her dad—but the place really grew on me. And I was touched to see that my aunt had been a gardener too. I felt a real connection with Patricia—something I never told anyone and probably never will…except for right here in the pages of this journal.

And when it was time to return to California, I felt very sad. Not that I let on. Over the years I have become quite a pro at concealing my feelings. In fact, I'm pretty sure I could be an actress. Not that I'd ever want to. Seriously, I can't think of anything more revolting. I would rather clean public toilets or sell faux designer purses on the sidewalk or, God forbid, flip hamburgers at McDonald's!

But as I sit here in my stuffy little attic room, I can't help but wish I were someone else…living somewhere else…with a different set of parents...and perhaps a friend or two. Unfortunately, I just don't think that's going to happen.

On another note, or perhaps simply as a distraction to my never-ending troubles, how about another earth-friendly suggestion for my someday green column. Sometimes I feel that caring about the planet is the only positive force in my entire life. Anyway, for what it's worth...

Maya's Green Tip for the Day

Most people turn on the bathroom faucet and let it run full blast to brush their teeth. Now what's up with all that nice clean water just rushing straight down the drain while you're standing there brushing your pearly whites? Why not simply wet your toothbrush, then turn off the water while you brush? Then turn the faucet back on to rinse your toothbrush and so on. Sure it takes a little more wrist energy, but that's a small price to pay for saving precious water. And if everyone did this, we would save millions of gallons of water each day.

Three

May 15

*S*hannon is gone again. This time she's been gone for three days. For all I know she could be dead. Now some people might think that I'd be glad if she was dead, but the truth is I wouldn't. I actually love my mom. I guess I just wish she loved me. And okay, I know she does…in her own dysfunctional way.

I'm sitting in her bedroom right now, perched on the worn cushion of the window seat, and writing in my journal. Shannon would be furious if she knew I was in here. Her bedroom is the one place in our house that is strictly off-limits to everyone, including me.

"It's my private oasis," she told me one day when I was very little and had wandered in. At the time I probably didn't know what that meant, but I heard it enough later to put two and two together. That was back when I had a full-time nanny, a sweet older woman named Jane. And as I recall, her skin was the same color as my dad's and just a few shades darker than my own. I had somehow escaped Nanny Jane's watchful eye that day, making it up the curving staircase and into my parents' bedroom. Correction—*Shannon's* bedroom. My dad had another room at the other end of the hallway, but I don't think I was aware of that yet. Back then my bedroom was downstairs, connected to Nanny Jane's room. And until that day, the first floor had been my entire world. Well, that and going outside for walks or playing in the yard. Going up the stairs was a whole new experience. But when I found I was unwelcome, I didn't go up again. Not for a few years anyway.

Now, as I look around my mom's "private oasis," I am surprised at how shabby and dirty it has become. The first time I saw this room, it seemed to sparkle with glistening gilt-framed mirrors and the shining glass-topped surfaces of polished antique furnishings, delicately arrayed with cut-crystal bottles of what I assume was perfume—or perhaps liquor. The room might've belonged to a fairy princess. Those were the days when we not only had a nanny but a housekeeper and a cook as well. The cook's name was Francesca, and the housekeeper was Rosa. I loved them all. And I actually thought they were part of our family. Probably because I saw them more than my parents.

But by the time I was five, the money was running out. Dad's records weren't selling, and no one was calling for gigs. This led to lots of fights between my parents, and one by one, Francesca, Rosa, and Nanny Jane all disappeared. I'm not sure if they quit or were fired. I just know that they all left within a very short period of time...and that I missed them desperately. Especially Nanny Jane. She was the only one who actually told me good-bye. And even when she did, I couldn't believe she was never coming back.

"You're too old for a nanny," my mom had told me. Then when my dad questioned this, along with her ability to care for her own child, it resulted in a huge fight. I didn't stick around to listen to the accusations tossed back and forth, but I heard them enough times over the next couple of years to learn them by heart. She would tell him he was a "washed-up, has-been blankity-blank," and he would point out that she was a "blanking useless blank." Nice things like that. The only thing I could count on between those two was that things would get worse.

I find it ironic that Shannon still keeps photos of my dad, although they are only displayed in her room. It does seem a bit odd, considering how she claims to hate his guts. In fact, she even keeps a handgun in here somewhere, and I've heard her say she might use it on him someday. To be fair, she only makes this claim when she's intoxicated or coming down from a bad high...or when he's extra late sending money. Over the years I've learned not to take her threats too seriously.

My favorite photo in here was taken when I was six. And although life at home was pretty messed up by then, you wouldn't know it to look at this picture. It was taken at the studio where my dad always had his album covers shot, and for some unknown reason, Shannon wanted a family photo. I think it was because she was about to turn forty, or so she claimed. Anyway, she insisted we dress up. Although the glass covering the photo is coated with dust, I can see that Dad had on a dark gray suit with a pale blue shirt and a striped tie. And he looks incredibly handsome. But it's his smile that gets me. It looks so genuine, and his eyes are so bright and clear, like he was really happy. It's the same expression I used to see when he'd pick me up and lift me high over his head and fly me around the yard like Peter Pan.

Shannon looks surprisingly happy too. She was wearing a gauzy, pale pink dress with what I think were real diamonds, long gone by now. She seems so dainty and delicate—pale blond hair as fluffy as cotton candy and her wide blue eyes with several coats of mascara to make the lashes appear thick and long. Or maybe she had on false eyelashes. She does that sometimes. But the general effect reminds me of a fairy princess, the type of person who might have once inhabited this room, back when it looked magical too.

And there I am, sitting in front of them, right in the middle of the photo. I was also wearing a pink dress. And I'm the only one in the photo not smiling. Not that I am frowning exactly. It's more a look of wonderment—or perhaps I was feeling hopeful, as if I thought that getting this happy family photo taken was a good omen for us. If so, I was wrong.

I study my dress, trying to remember how the fabric felt. It was soft cotton with rosebuds embroidered along the hem, probably a Laura Ashley. And although the dress was sweet, it wasn't nearly as pretty or as pale a pink as Shannon's. And of course, my hair, eyes, and skin were not as pale as hers either. I know I am a combination of my parents—part Caucasian and part African American—yet it's my dad's black heritage that I've related to most over the years. In many ways Shannon feels like a stranger to me.

And as I notice my reflection in one of the many mirrors in this room, I realize that I look like a stranger in here too. I stand out against the pale blue walls, and my overalls look dark and out of place against the faded blue and white fabric of the window seat. Everything, from my curly, dark brown hair to my almost-black eyes to my "almond-colored complexion," as Shannon calls it, does not belong in my mother's bedroom. I am too dark. I don't look a bit like my mother's daughter.

I wonder if that's part of the reason she sometimes seems to despise me. Yet it was her choice to marry my father. Although occasionally I wonder if she married his fame and fortune as much as she married him. Because once that was gone, or appeared to be gone, she seemed to despise him as well. Or maybe she simply despises herself.

I wonder where she is right now...and if she's okay. Although I seriously doubt she is "okay." Not in the real sense of the word. I guess the most I can hope for is that she's alive. I'm tempted to e-mail my dad again. This time I would tell him the truth—that Shannon is a mess, that she's doing drugs again, that she's been gone for three days, and that I'm almost out of money (from my secret stash I keep hidden from her). But I'm afraid it will upset him to hear these things. And it's important for him to stay focused just now. He's mentioned several times how vital it is for him to invest all of himself and all of his energy and talent into his career right now. I don't want to be the reason he fails; that would ruin everything for all of us.

I look at an old photo of my dad. It's on Shannon's bedside table, partially buried amid the clutter piled around it—old dusty magazines, empty prescription bottles, a Jack Daniel's bottle on its side, and a couple of dirty glasses next to it, along with a lacy black bra that's seen better days. I'm tempted to do some cleaning in here, but that would only create more trouble when Shannon comes home. If she comes home, that is.

Anyway, I study Dad's picture. It must've been a publicity photo because it's a head-and-shoulders shot with his chin tilted slightly down. He has a partial smile, and those sparkling dark eyes seem to be holding a little something back—a secret perhaps. I'm sure this was taken when Nick Stark was at the height of his career, when his name was a household word and his albums were selling like hot cakes.

Probably before I was born, back when my parents thought the money would never stop pouring in.

As I look at this shot, I can see why Shannon might've truly fallen in love with my dad. It could've had as much to do with his looks and charm and wit and generosity as his fame and fortune. Anyway, I'd like to think that.

It's hard to believe that so much was lost—and over a relatively short time too, although it seemed longer back when I was little. But after the final fight and my dad moving out, our standard of living plunged steadily. I realize that both my parents are to blame for this. My dad, depressed and angry over the breakup of his marriage, became increasingly reckless and irresponsible with his finances. According to Shannon, he squandered millions. But I think that's an exaggeration—and probably her way of getting the spotlight off her and all the money she wasted on cocaine. For all I know, that could've been millions too.

Shannon used to blame Dad for her addiction problems, and I suppose that's partially true since he admitted to me that it was one of his music connections who originally brought cocaine into our home. But the truth of the matter is, Nick Stark has always avoided drugs, even marijuana—a habit Shannon didn't attempt to hide from anyone. Whether it was in our backyard or the living room, my mom wasn't afraid to just light up when the mood hit her. "It soothes my shattered nerves," she would say to anyone who questioned her. As if her lifestyle was so very stressful.

Of course, this aggravated my dad. His father was also a musician—and a heroin addict, who died young. I believe that put a genuine fear into Dad's heart, because to this day he abhors all drugs. I guess my only question is, why does he knowingly allow me to remain with a woman who uses and abuses substances like cocaine and amphetamines? But I know the answer, and it's threefold: (1) there's a lot of denial going on, (2) my dad does not like to engage in any unnecessary conflict with Shannon, and (3) he's just too busy.

Even so, I wonder what Nick Stark's fans would think if they knew his fifteen-year-old daughter is fending for herself while her mom is out on a three-day drug binge (well, three days so far). Then again, maybe no one would care. After all, this is not a new story. In some ways I can really relate to Nicole Richie. Her story is freakily similar to mine. And yet when Nicole blows it (by being anorexic or drunk and disorderly or whatever...) and she makes the front page, it seems as if everyone takes potshots at her. They call her "shallow" and "spoiled" and say she has "entitlement issues." It's like no one remembers how she was raised, the things she's been through. Why doesn't anyone care to attribute some of her problems to the fact that she grew up in a very strange family? But then again, maybe it's really not so strange. Not by my standards anyway.

Sometimes I wonder if the way I'm living might actually be turning into the norm in this country. Maybe it's simply my fantasy that there are healthy, happy, well-adjusted families out there. Moms who drive kids to soccer and ballet. Dads who come home for dinner. Perhaps a dog or a cat running around. Food in the fridge. Utility bills that are paid. Am I wrong to assume that people like my cousin Kim and her dad are the norm? What if they're the anomaly?

Even so, more and more I find myself wanting what they have. It's like a desperate craving, a deep, pathetic longing that will never be fulfilled. Because I can never have what Kim and her dad have—what their little family had before Kim's mom died. It's completely out of my reach. I'm like the poor little kid with her nose pushed against the toy store window, just wishing. Only it's not the toys I want. The sad truth is, I've actually had more than my fair share of that kind of junk. When I was little, my dad used to bring home all kinds of things to make up for being gone so much. Nanny Jane was always picking things up and complaining that my room looked more like a toy store than a nursery. And later on, after the divorce, when I'd go to visit Dad, he would use the latest video games and electronic gadgets to pay me off. Only it never worked.

I've had all the material things any kid could want. But that doesn't make up for what I haven't had, and that doesn't make me want it less. And writing in this stupid journal only seems to make me feel worse! I think Kim was wrong about the therapy thing. Although writing about the earth is kind of therapeutic for me. So here goes.

Maya's Green Tip for the Day

The three basic rules for green living are: reduce, reuse, and recycle. Today I'll talk to you about the first rule. To reduce, you simply make a conscious decision to <u>consume less</u>. That means you don't buy without thinking. Before you make a purchase, ask yourself: (1) do you really need that item, (2) do you already have something that can serve the same purpose, and (3) can you buy that item in a recycled form and/or recycle it when you're finished with it? Like instead of buying a new bike, maybe you can find a good secondhand bike. Also, to be really green, you should ask yourself if the item you're buying will last a long time and whether it's made from renewable resources (things that grow, like bamboo or cotton or domestic woods) and where and how it was made (like did they waste energy to make it?).

Four

May 31

Yes, it's been a while since I picked up a pen to record what's been going on in my life...and in this particular nut house. But let me start by saying this has been the worst month of my life. And if you knew everything about my life, you would know that means it's been bad. Seriously bad. That's the main reason I've avoided writing in my journal the past couple of weeks. It's just too depressing. Even for me. But suddenly I feel the need to document these things. Perhaps I can use this journal in court as evidence of my mom's inability to parent.

Shannon has been a complete yo-yo the last three weeks. She's like the human roller-coaster ride. She does a two- to three-day missing act, which I know is related to a partying drug binge, and then she comes home completely wiped out. It takes her a day or so to recover, and then she puts on this act like everything is back to normal. As if we even know "normal."

Lately she's even made some pathetic attempts to cook meals for us, which is a big joke—not to mention an enormous mess that I usually have to clean up. But during her recovery time, she promises that she's not going to pull this stuff again. She says things like "I make myself sick!" and "I can't keeping living like this!" And she asks me to help her, sometimes breaking down in tears, begging me to stand by her. Naturally, I say that I will. But even as I make these promises, I'm not sure I can keep them. I've learned from the best that promises are made to be broken.

Still, she almost had me convinced a couple of weeks ago. I'd been considering calling my dad to ask for help. But that night Shannon sobbed and swore that it was her last time and that her "problem" was going to stop and that she was ready to get professional help. So a few sober days passed, and I did begin to feel a smidgen of hope.

I got into my routine of doing schoolwork, hoping to finish this year and take the summer off like other kids. And just when I felt like my feet were back on the ground, Shannon jerked the rug right out from under me and took off again. She told me she was going to NA (Narcotics Anonymous), which actually turned out to be true. But when she finally came home two days later, she confessed that she'd hooked up with an old coke buddy and that they'd gone out partying following the NA meeting. How's that for networking?

Then a few days ago, shortly after the check from Dad finally arrived, she took off again. At least I'd had the smarts to insist on going to the bank with her. After cashing the check, she handed me two hundred dollars to go shopping. Yeah, right. The only place I shop these days is the grocery store, where I buy exciting things like biodegradable toilet paper, environmentally friendly laundry soap, and organic food. Then when Shannon finally came home last night, she was (big surprise here) totally broke.

"Have you got any money, baby?" she asked in that slurred and scratchy pathetic voice that sounds like she's still under the influence. I told her, "Sorry," that I was broke too, which was, of course, a lie. A self-preservation lie. After that, she closed herself up in her room, and I haven't seen her since. Not that I care. I am beginning to care less and less... about everything.

I just don't know how long I can go on like this. Seriously, I feel like giving up. And I felt so desperate this morning that I actually e-mailed my cousin Kim, asking for advice. I told her a little—just a teeny, tiny bit—about what's going on in my life these days. Of course, immediately after hitting Send, I regretted my confession. I wish I could've retrieved the e-mail, but I don't think that's possible. Anyway, I haven't heard back from her yet. I suspect her life is fairly busy. Or maybe my message got lost somewhere in cyberspace. Sometimes that's how my life feels to me—lost in space.

I guess the part that scares me most—as far as Kim having a glimpse into my life—is that I don't really know this girl. Oh, sure, she's my cousin. Not that it counts for anything.

I mean, her mom, my aunt, seemed like a nice person, but Kim is a complete unknown factor to me. What if she can't be trusted? And yet I've just divulged a pretty huge secret to her. What if she tells her dad and they decide to do something really, really stupid—like call L.A. County DCFS? I've gone down the road with Children and Family Services before, and I didn't like where it took me.

When I was thirteen, I actually looked into getting emancipated from Shannon. Things were bad then...but not as bad as now. Naturally, Shannon threw a total hissy fit—she would lose out financially if I was emancipated. No more big checks from my dad. So before the caseworker could come to our house and check things out, Shannon went to a lot of work to put on the appearance of "normal." Well, as normal as anyone in L.A. might be. And don't forget, the woman is an actress. And her act was convincing. Not that it mattered, because as the caseworker politely pointed out, I wasn't old enough to be emancipated yet. According to her, the law states that not only must your parents sign off, but you must have a place to live and be able to continue attending school as well as have a job that can support you. Well, duh. What thirteen-year-old can support herself? I mean, besides by heading down to Wilshire Boulevard and selling my body for sex. Like that's going to happen!

At the time I investigated emancipation, my dad was just beginning to tour again. And naturally, he wasn't interested in taking me along for the ride. It didn't help that Shannon, still in actress mode, had somehow convinced him that I was "simply experiencing a bad case of teenage angst." She even asked him if he'd seen that film *Thirteen*. Give me a break! I mean, it's an interesting movie, but those two girls pretty much go nuts.

Eventually, my caseworker told me that if my home life was really so terrible, my best option might be to get on a waiting list for a group foster home. Okay, I've heard about the foster-care system in our state, and that scared me even more than living with Shannon. So I just shut my mouth and decided to bide my time. Now I'm wondering if fifteen is old enough to be emancipated. But then there's that pesky job thing and those other legal details. Still, it might be worth looking into. Although it would help if I were sixteen and could drive. Unfortunately, my birthday isn't until December.

Even so, I wonder if I could get a job. There are places close enough to walk or ride my bike to, but would they hire a fifteen-year-old? Although I've been told I look old for my age.

June 5

After searching online and the classifieds and after making a few inquiries, I quickly discovered that the only places fifteen-year-olds can find work in our neighborhood is at fast-food restaurants or by doing yard work, housecleaning, or baby-sitting. I cannot work in a restaurant, because I refuse to handle animal by-products. I would gladly do yard work, but so far no one has returned my calls. I think it's because I'm a girl, which seems like discrimination to me. Speaking of discrimination, when I called about housecleaning, the woman spoke to me in Spanish, and even though my Spanish is okay for a gringa, she didn't sound the least bit interested in interviewing me. They probably only hire Latinos. And my only experience with baby-sitting was when our neighbors' eighteen-month-old grandbabies came to visit last summer. The twin boys, Liam and Rye, were adorable, from a distance anyway, but after two weeks of changing diapers and chasing down screaming toddlers, well, I still cannot bear to think of it.

If I'm going to work toward being on my own, I need to find work. And based on Shannon's erratic behavior this past month, I need to make a plan. So on my way to the Market Basket, my favorite natural food store (who is not hiring), I notice a Help Wanted sign in the window of a rather chichi clothing boutique. Now honestly, the last thing I want to do is sell overpriced designer clothes to over-spending, undernourished, shopaholic women (not unlike my mom), but maybe they just want a stock girl. That might not be too torturous.

So I hurry to gather my tofu products, nuts, a fresh loaf of vegan bread, and organically grown fruit, and I carefully pack these groceries into my reusable canvas Earth bag and come directly home, put them away, and then begin to make a plan.

Shannon, once again, is gone. I had hoped it was just an ordinary date, since the guy who picked her up seemed halfway decent, but when she didn't make it home, I had to assume she was out getting high again. In a way, this is lucky, because this allows me to borrow a few things from her packed closet—a walk-in closet that's bigger than some people's bedrooms. Although she has all kinds of storage, things are heaped in piles, and she won't even notice if a few items go missing.

It's not as if I don't have clothes that would be appropriate for working in a clothing boutique. I have lots of things I never even wear—"stylish" rags that Shannon gets me whether I want them or not. Drugs aren't her only addiction. But after checking out my closet, I know I need to bring it up a notch or two. I am not stupid. As soon as I walk into that boutique and ask for a job application, eyes will be narrowed, and my outfit will be scrutinized. And I know that I have to measure up to their shallow standards.

Okay, part of me is screaming, *Why are you doing this, Maya? Why are you compromising yourself? Why are you becoming a hypocrite?* I mean, not only am I willing to work in a business I do not respect. I am willing to carry a bag made of leather! What is wrong with this picture? The answer is simple: I'm desperate. I'm nearly broke again. This is the first step in my emancipation plan, so I'll bite the bullet and just do it.

June 6

Picking up the application actually went fairly smoothly today. A stick-thin woman named Em was friendly enough. She had short, choppy hair that was dyed jet black and tipped with midnight blue.

"We can use some help right now," she told me as she set some white boxes down beside the register. No one else was in the shop just then. "Have you worked in retail before?"

"No." I gave her my most confident smile. "Well, other than shopping."

She laughed as she handed me an application. "Make sure you put that on your application. Vivian takes customers more seriously than employees."

"Vivian?"

"The owner. She's at lunch, but she should be back by two."

"Should I fill this out here and then wait…do you think?" Suddenly I realized how inept I am at this sort of thing. I am clueless. What is a person supposed to do to get a job?

"I don't know…" Em frowned at her red plastic watch. "Viv's two can sometimes turn into three or four. Why don't you take the application and fill it out at your convenience, then drop it by later?"

I nodded. "Sure, of course." I adjusted the strap of Shannon's Dolce & Gabbana purse over my shoulder and stood straighter.

"Great bag," Em said.

"D 'n' G," I said, sounding more like Shannon than ever.

"Great belt too."

Now I was stumped. I couldn't remember the designer. "Gucci?"

"Oh yeah," I said casually, like no big deal. Still, this whole designer name game is so ludicrous. I can't believe I'm even willing to play.

"See you 'round," she called out as I headed for the door.

So, feeling slightly reassured, I raced home. Okay, I didn't race straightaway. The first thing I did, once I got a few doors down the street, was remove the three-inch-heel sandals, which were cutting into my feet (they, too, are Gucci and a half size too small since they're Shannon's). I slipped them into the bag and pulled out a well-worn pair of flip-flops instead. Now, I can't believe these "experts" who are saying that flip-flops aren't good for your feet. I mean, have they tried wearing three-inch heels? And maybe they don't know the difference between the Payless kind of flip-flops and Earth Shoe flip-flops. Anyway, with happier feet I hurried home, where I carefully filled out the application, using my neatest penmanship and exaggerating my job experience and education. I actually wrote "retail sales experience in the music industry" as one of my jobs because I used to help my dad sell CDs at his gigs. I even listed Nick Stark as my employer. Hopefully this Vivian person wouldn't go over the application too carefully. And I must admit, it looked impressive to have more blanks filled in.

I waited until three thirty, and then after checking my hair and makeup (wouldn't my mom be proud!), I headed back down to Rodeo Drive and the chichi boutique that I normally wouldn't be caught dead in. And to be fair, it's not actually on Rodeo Drive proper—it's on a side street. Still, it felt wrong. So wrong.

The shop, once again, was empty. Once again, the soft jazz music played, and the air conditioner felt way too cold. If I got hired there, I would try to sneak the thermostat up a few degrees.

This time Em was standing by the cash register looking slightly bored. "You're back," she said cheerfully.

"Yes." I took a deep breath and focused on appearing older than I was as I held up my application form. "I have my application all filled out." Okay, that's a big *duh*.

"Vivian," she called over her shoulder, "here's the girl I told you about."

An older woman, fortyish, came out of the back room. Her hair was long and straight and about the color of a pomegranate. Suddenly I wondered if you had to dye your hair to work here. In that case, I wasn't interested. A girl could only go so far. This woman peered curiously at me from behind narrow, purple-rimmed glasses.

"Hello," I said in what I hoped sounded like a professional yet friendly tone. "I'm Maya." I held out my application again, but she didn't make the slightest move to take it. Instead, she just stared at me, like she was literally taking an inventory. I felt certain that I must not be measuring up. I wanted to turn and run.

Finally she spoke in a sharp tone. "Have you worked in sales before?"

I smiled nervously and moved toward her. "Yes. It's on my application." I sort of waved the paper in front of her, then realized that was stupid. Okay, I was in over my head, and I knew it.

She moved to the side of the counter but was still staring at me like I was an exhibit at the San Diego Zoo. Was this how zebras feel?

"She's also a shopper," Em said, obviously trying to be helpful. "Isn't that a great bag she's got there?"

Without moving her eyes from my face, Vivian nodded, then slowly took my application from me with her thumb and forefinger, as if it might be contaminated. Feeling like I'd invaded her space, I took a quick step backward, but the heel of my sandal caught on a thick Oriental runner in front of the counter, and I nearly fell. Fortunately I caught myself on the edge of the counter, but I upset a basket of beaded bracelets as I did this little acrobatic act.

"Sorry," I muttered as I knelt to pick up the bracelets. I took my time to carefully return them to the basket, arranging them like a beaded rainbow and not looking up, although I knew they both were staring at me. All I wanted was to get out of there ASAP. But I simply stood and put the basket back on the counter. Avoiding Vivian's eyes, I thanked her for her time and began to make my way to the door.

"Bye," Em called in a less hopeful voice. Vivian said nothing.

Well, that's that. I took my time walking home. I felt hopeless. But I was barely in the door of my house when my cell phone rang. Assuming it was Shannon and hoping it wasn't anything serious, I quickly answered.

"Maya Stark?" said a sharp-toned female voice.

"Yes?"

"This is Vivian Demarco."

It was the woman I'd just humiliated myself in front of, and I timidly said, "Yes?" again.

"I noticed on your application that you say you worked for Nick Stark."

"That's correct."

"I also noticed that your last name is Stark... Are you any relation?"

"He's my dad."

Then it was silent on her end, and I wondered if she thought I was lying. "Look, you probably don't want—"

"I'd like to schedule you for an interview tomorrow morning. Around ten thirty?"

"Sure," I said quickly. "That's fine."

"See you then." And she hung up.

So there you go. One minute you're ready to give up on something completely, and the next thing you know, you're getting a second chance. This actually kind of relates to my next green tip.

Maya's Green Tip for the Day

The second green rule is reuse. Most Americans like things that are disposable, meaning you use it once, then toss it. For instance, disposable diapers—they may make a mommy's life easier, but they really fill up the landfill sites. Unfortunately, most mommies would never consider using cloth diapers. Besides that, do you know how many grocery bags are used once and thrown away each day? Millions! That's why I take my reusable canvas bag to get groceries. Not only is it "green"; it never tears. But even if you don't use a canvas bag, you can still recycle grocery sacks by giving them a second go-round (like as a garbage can liner) or simply returning the bags to the store to be used for groceries again. Hey, every little bit helps.

Five

June 7

Shannon came home late last night. As usual, she didn't say a word to me, just slipped into her room like all was well. Still feeling slightly stunned that I had a job interview with Vivian in the morning, I didn't feel as concerned about Shannon as I usually would. Perhaps working would be a good diversion for me.

When I got up this morning, Shannon was still holed up in her room. No surprises there. But that was fine with me, since I had borrowed a couple more items from her yesterday. Hoping to make a good impression on Vivian, I snatched a paisley blouse with a label called What Comes Around Goes Around (seriously, that's the name of the designer, and it seems to be appropriate) as well as another pair of shoes, a pair of cork wedge slides by Prada (I'm trying to memorize the names). I put these together with a slim brown skirt with a designer name I can't even pronounce and gold-toned costume jewelry that seemed like something Vivian might approve of.

I felt like a complete phony as I sneaked out of the house. Even with the Prada shoes still in my bag, I felt more like my mom than myself as I slunk down the driveway. I hadn't worn anything made of leather for nearly two years, and here for the second day in a row, I'd compromised myself like this. Truly sickening! As I walked down the hill (wearing my flip-flops to preserve my feet), I felt I was about one step from going out and prostituting myself on Hollywood Boulevard. Seriously, I felt like I'd lost it.

Not that it stopped me. With visions of earning my own money, getting my own car—hopefully a hybrid—and having my own place to live, and finally being free from Shannon, I was a driven woman! And as I marched down Rodeo Drive, I felt like I could even eat meat. Okay, that's probably an exaggeration. But I was determined, ready to do whatever it took to get myself to a better place.

At 10:25 I stopped at the same bench where I'd changed my shoes yesterday, and making sure that Vivian was nowhere in sight, I quickly slipped on the Prada slides, trying to ignore the soft strips of brown suede (and that some poor cow had sacrificed itself for these stupid shoes). Then after pausing to catch my breath and center myself, I carefully proceeded to the boutique. I hadn't considered the height of these wedge heels. They must be more than four inches, which probably makes me about six feet tall. But I was thinking, *Hey, I may be only fifteen, but at least I'm taller than Vivian and Em.* Then I reminded myself to watch my step on those Oriental carpets. *Balance, it's all about balance.*

"Vivian said to go into her office," Em said as soon as I came in. "It's the red door back there."

So watching my step, I went through a small back room and knocked on a shiny red door, then cautiously opened it after I heard a female voice calling, "Come in."

"Hello?" I peered in to see a shiny black enamel desk offset by a couple of red leather chairs. In one corner was an Asian folding screen of black silk with a red embroidered dragon on it. But as far as I could see, no one was there. "Hello..."

"Just. Sit. Down," called a rather uptight-sounding voice from behind the screen. I assumed it belonged to Vivian.

So I sat in a leather chair and waited until she finally emerged wearing a fitted sleeveless dress with a bright geometric pattern. "Help me with this zipper," she commanded as she turned her back to me.

I hurried to get up and zip the snug dress. "That's pretty," I said, although I actually thought it was pretty ugly. *Hypocrite. Liar. Phony.*

She turned and held out her arms as if to model it. "It's a new design from What Comes Around Goes Around."

Without batting an eyelash, I said, "I thought so." Another lie. "Same as my blouse."

She narrowed her eyes, as if to scrutinize me, then finally nodded. "Very nice." She pointed to a chair. "Now sit."

Feeling like a trained dog, I sat.

"Okay, Maya, let's get right to it. You're only fifteen. Do you have a work permit?"

"Well, no..."

"And you're really Nick Stark's daughter..." She said this more like a statement than a question, so I simply waited. "I know this for a fact because I did some checking on you."

"Oh..."

"My question is, why does Nick Stark's daughter want to work here?"

I forced a smile. "I thought it would be fun. And good experience. I want to learn more about fashion." *Lies. Lies. Lies.*

"Well, you seem smart. And I've been a Nick Stark fan since the eighties."

I smiled with a bit more confidence. "I'm a hard worker."

She looked doubtful. "Well, you're a pretty girl. And very fashionable. I'm willing to give you a try." Then she handed me another form. "That's for a work permit. Get it taken care of, and I'll see how you do."

"You mean I'm hired?"

"Em will train you. I'd like you to start tomorrow if you can get your work permit. I'm expecting a busy weekend."

"Tomorrow?" I blinked in surprise.

"Are you telling me you don't work on Saturdays?"

"No, that's not what I meant."

"Because I don't need any princesses working for me,

Maya. Just because you have a famous father doesn't mean I want you to go around here acting like Paris Hilton."

"No, of course not."

"We open at ten."

"Is that when I'm supposed to be here?"

"Have I been unclear?"

"Not at all." Okay, that was another big fat lie. I still felt pretty confused.

Vivian stood now, as if she was done. Then she suddenly paused to look directly into my face. "By the way, I hope you're not a thief."

"Of course not."

She looked skeptical. "Most of the girls who've worked for me have tried to steal from me at one time or another. But I have hidden cameras. I always catch them." She narrowed her eyes. "And I always prosecute."

"Don't worry, I'm not a thief," I said quickly.

"Let's hope not."

Then I thanked her and was about to leave.

"How tall are you?" she demanded suddenly.

I turned to look at her, then shrugged. "I don't know."

"You don't *know*?"

"Well...the last time I was measured I was about five-six." I didn't admit that I was only thirteen at the time.

She laughed in a harsh way. Was there some sort of height requirement in her shop? Perhaps she was accustomed to hiring short girls with colorfully dyed hair. Maybe she hadn't really offered me a job after all.

"Is my height a problem?" I asked, suddenly slumping. Then I pointed to the tall wedges of my Prada slides. "These make me a lot taller. I could wear flats if you like."

She gave me a look that suggested she was questioning my sanity, or maybe she was wondering if I'd dropped down to Earth from a different planet. Mars perhaps.

"Your shoes are fine," she said in a bored tone. "Good day."

Feeling excused, I hurried out. Vivian would never be a candidate for Miss Congeniality. On the other hand, I've had lots of experience with difficult people. Beginning with my mother.

"How'd it go?" Em asked when I emerged.

"Okay..." I spoke quietly, noticing that a couple of shoppers were looking at shoes.

"Did you get it?"

I gave her the thumbs-up. "Vivian said that you're supposed to train me, and it looks like I'll start tomorrow." Then I held up the work-permit form. "That is, if I can get this taken care of, although I'm not really sure what needs to be done."

So she explained that all I needed was to fill out the blanks on the form and then have my mom go with me to the employment division to verify her signature. "Easy breezy. I had to do one, too, a few years ago."

I tried not to look alarmed about this bit of news. Shannon had to go to the employment division today? Like that was going to happen. I thanked Em and told her I'd see her tomorrow but seriously doubted I would. I walked a few doors down and sat on what was becoming a familiar bench. Maybe I should give it a name, like Harry or Ben or maybe Bernard. Yes, Bernard the Bench.

So I sat on Bernard and switched out Shannon's Pradas for my comfy flip-flops. Then I took time to read through the work-permit application, thinking maybe it wasn't as hopeless as I'd assumed. But when I finished perusing the form, I knew it was impossible. For starters, the employment division wanted to know about my schooling. Where I had attended, with dates. What was I supposed to put there? More challenging, how would I get Shannon out of the house? And how was she going to be fit to drive me downtown to the employment division, not to mention stand before a witness to sign a legal document? No, I just wasn't feeling it.

On the other hand, if I didn't show up for work in the morning, I could kiss that job good-bye. Finally, as I slowly walked back up the hill toward my house, I knew my only option would be blackmail. I would tell Shannon that if she didn't take me down to the employment division today and if she didn't sign that paper, I would call Dad and tell him everything—in detail!

"I'm sick," she complained when I told her she needed to drive me somewhere. I had decided not to give her all the details at once.

"Trust me, I know." I handed her a glass of watered-down ginger ale. It's about the only thing she can handle at times like this. "But you have to go."

"Why?" Her voice was scratchy and thin, almost like a little kid's.

So I told her about my job opportunity.

She almost looked sober as she blinked her bloodshot eyes. "You got a job?"

I nodded. "Yes. I start tomorrow. But you have to sign this paper in front of a witness at the employment division." By then I had already filled out the application. And following my mom's fine example, I had lied on the lines about schooling. I made it appear as if I'd continued in public schooling and was now out for summer break. Hopefully the high school would be closed by now and no one would be the wiser.

Anyway, I had nothing to lose. Also, I knew that Shannon would never read the application. I'd be lucky if I could get her into the car. My plan was to drive. Okay, I don't have my learner's permit yet, but I should. I'm old enough. And I already know how to drive. Well, sort of. I've driven Shannon's car numerous times. Of course, this was usually in an emergency, like when she was too drunk or high to drive. Or it was nighttime, and we needed food, and she handed me the keys. Still, I figured we'd be safer with me behind the wheel this afternoon.

Incredibly, after much coaxing, guilt tripping, and threatening, I finally have Shannon cleaned up and dressed and sitting in the passenger seat. Sure, she looks slightly zombielike just now. Her skin looks paler than usual behind her oversize dark glasses. But hopefully she'll perk up when the coffee kicks in. I made her drink two mugs of espresso.

It took most of the afternoon to get us to the employment office, and it's about ten minutes before closing time when my number is finally called. I drag Shannon up to the counter, where a balding, middle-aged man on the other side looks tired and grizzled. And something about the way he adjusts his wire-rimmed glasses and peers at me suggests that he has less than zero patience by now. Even so, I smile innocently at him as I nudge Shannon forward and give her a look that says, *You'd better get with it, lady, or you'll be sorry.*

After a long pause, she comes to life. Amazingly, she kicks it into high gear, and as I watch her performance, I think perhaps she could make a comeback as an actress after all.

"Hello there, Mr. Blankenship," she says cheerfully, actually pausing to read his photo ID nametag, which is more than I had even hoped for. "I'm Shannon Stark, and this is my daughter, Maya. She's just landed a sweet little job in one of the coolest boutiques on Rodeo Drive, and if you could just witness my signature on this work permit, we'll let you get on with your weekend." She gives him one of her coy, flashy smiles now. "I'm sure you've got some great plans too."

Well, just like magic, he warms right up, and barely skimming the application, he nods, then watches with interest as she signs on the line. He does what needs to be done, and before I know it, we're outta there.

Of course, as soon as we're in the car, Shannon slumps down in the passenger side like a deflated balloon. *"I'm dying,"* she says dramatically.

"You'll be home soon," I promise. But thanks to the commuter traffic, it takes an hour and a half, and by the time I pull into our driveway, I feel like I'm dying too.

"Oh, we're here already?" Shannon looks up at the house in surprise. She's been asleep the whole time.

I get out of the car and don't even wait for her. I feel a mixture of emotions as I stomp into the house. On one hand, I'm proud that I accomplished all I did today. On the other hand, I'm outraged that—thanks to my parents—I am doing some outrageous things. Like breaking the law by driving without a permit and lying about my schooling, and how about compromising my convictions by wearing leather?! I do all this just to survive—just so I can hopefully reach the place where I can be free of Shannon and her madness. Still, it is so not fair. But that only proves my belief that (1) life is not fair, and (2) it is not going to get better. So why freak over it?

Tonight I retreat to the attic to escape Shannon. This time I take a few survival things, including food and water, my laptop and sketchbook, and this journal. I'm amazed at how this journal is beginning to feel like a friend. Maybe Kim was right after all. Maybe it is therapeutic.

And when I checked my e-mail about an hour ago, I was surprised to see she had finally written me back. I can tell that her life has been a little crazy too. She tells me "in confidence" that her best friend is pregnant. Now that's kind of shocking. Anyway, it seems that Kim has been helping this girl sort things out, and it's getting kind of stressful. I feel sorry for Kim and think I shouldn't tell her too much more about my situation. But she also encourages me to be in touch with my dad. I think she assumes that he is something like her dad—that he'll care about me and want to do something to change my living conditions.

Well, that just shows you how someone's personal perspective can impair their worldview. To be fair, I suppose that my world is as foreign to her as hers is to me. But it was kind of her to write. I decide to write back and act as if all is well. This girl has enough stuff on her plate without me adding my mess to the mix.

Speaking of messes, some people think that it's messy to wash out and flatten cans, but recycling helps to keep the earth clean.

Maya's Green Tip for the Day

So here's the third green rule: recycle. That means you don't just toss something into the trash because you're done with it. Besides the fact that our landfills are overflowing, we're also running out of some resources, like oils that are used to make plastic. So if you make an effort to separate recyclable products like glass, metal, plastic, and paper, we all benefit. Sure, this takes a little time, but isn't the planet worth it?

Six

June 8

I'm only fifteen, and this was my first day at my first job. I should feel elated, right? Wrong. *Deflated* would be more like it. And tired. And my feet hurt. I mean, seriously hurt. Can wearing these stupid shoes do permanent damage to your feet? I asked Em about wearing flip-flops in the boutique, and she just frowned. No way would I ask Vivian. She'd probably slap me. Not that she's violent, not physically anyway, but she is definitely mean.

Like this morning. A customer was perusing the summer dresses, and I was "trying to help her." Actually I was standing around looking like an idiot. The woman—a petite, anorexic, fortyish blonde with wrinkly, tanned skin—wanted something special for a graduation party tonight. At first I tried to make some suggestions, but I could tell I was only irritating her. I could also tell I was being watched by Vivian. And since I wanted to appear useful and like I was worth the minimum wage I was earning, or hoping to earn if I didn't get fired on my first day, I stayed close by. I held up some dresses that I actually thought might look nice on her, but she wasn't buying. Eventually the skinny blonde left without making a purchase.

"You're not supposed to prey on the customers," Vivian snapped at me as soon as the shop was void of shoppers.

"Sorry," I muttered.

"Give them their space. Be helpful but invisible."

"Invisible?"

"Stay out of their way!" Then she flitted off to the back room where I assume she smoked several cigarettes since I could smell smoke when I went back for a potty break.

So later today, when Em was on her break, I was attempting to take Vivian's advice. I was trying to be "helpful but invisible" when three girls came into the shop. They were about my age, and thankfully I didn't know them. They are the kind of girls who walk around with a serious superiority complex, acting as if their life calling is to make others feel as if they are dust beneath their feet. But putting all offense and personal feelings aside, I politely asked if I could help them with anything. This is exactly what Em does. But like most of the other customers today, they said, "No, we're just looking." Okay, they said it even more snootily than the women had. So I backed off.

At first I stayed a few racks away, pretending to straighten garments, putting the hangers a finger's width apart, like Em had shown me. Then I went over to the counter and refolded a stack of Hermès silk scarves that had been messed up by a previous customer. The girls spent at least fifteen minutes checking out the shop, laughing and acting like the stuck-up brats they obviously were, and finally, to my relief, they left.

"Maya!" Vivian shrieked as she emerged from the back room. "You let them get away!"

"Huh?"

"Go and get them." Vivian had a cell phone by her ear as she pointed at the door.

"What?"

"Go! Run out there, and get those little thieves, and bring them back here! Now!"

So without even considering how I was going to do this, and without remembering that I was wearing those detestable Gucci sandals that were already cutting into my toes, and without realizing that I would not be able to run and catch anyone, I took off. I got out onto the sidewalk and looked both ways, but those girls were nowhere to be seen. Like they'd vanished into thin air. I walked up and down the sidewalk, looking every which way, but could not see them anywhere. Finally I went back inside.

"Where are they?" Vivian demanded with the phone still by her ear.

"They're gone."

"You didn't catch them?"

I held up my hands, like, *Duh, do you see them anywhere on me?*

"Never mind," she said into the phone. "They got away." Then she hung up and glared at me. "Did you know those girls?"

"No, of course not." She didn't look convinced. "They really took something?"

"Do you think I'm making it up?"

"Well...no..."

"Why weren't you watching them?"

"Watching?"

"Yes. Why were you up here behind the counter just stand- ing around and doing nothing?"

"I was folding the—"

"Your job is to take care of the customers, Maya! Is that too difficult for you to grasp?"

"But you said—"

"I don't expect you to be hiding behind the counter when we have customers in the store. Is that clear?"

"Yes, but—"

"No buts!"

Just then Em came in. She seemed to sense something was wrong, but instead of saying a word, she simply slipped into the back room, probably to put away her purse, although she took her time about it.

"I'm sorry," I forced myself to say. "I'll try to do better."

"You do not *try* to do better, Maya. You make a choice to do better."

"You're right," I said calmly, thinking of how much this reminded me of past nonsensical conversations with Shannon. "I will do better."

"Hello," Em said in a slightly timid tone. "Everything okay?"

Vivian glared at her now. "Maya just let some girls shoplift."

I literally bit my tongue. I "let" them?

Em just nodded. "That's too bad."

"I'll say," snapped Vivian as she headed back toward the shoe section. "They took a pair of Fendi sandals." She held up an empty box. "That dumpy redhead slipped them right under her shirt."

I tried to remember the "dumpy redhead" and what kind of shirt she'd been wearing but came up blank. "You saw that on a security camera?" I asked, instantly realizing how stupid I must sound.

Vivian gave me the evil eye. "No, Maya, I have x-ray vision. I can see through walls." Then shoving the empty shoebox at me, she turned and stomped off toward the back room. "I should deduct them from your wages."

I looked at the price on the box and tried not to gasp. I am not a math whiz, but at $7.50 an hour, it would take more than two weeks to pay back $680. "Would she really do that?" I whispered to Em.

"No," Em replied quietly, "that's illegal."

I let out a small sigh. Even so, I felt like I'd better stay on my toes. My poor aching toes! And later on when more teen girls came into the shop, I still tried to be invisible, but I did not let them out of my sight. Fortunately, they left without stealing anything. At least nothing I heard about from Vivian, although she might've been out of her office by then. Of course, they didn't buy anything either. I'm not sure if that was my fault or not. Working in an expensive boutique feels like walking a tightrope in uncomfortable shoes. I'm not sure how long I'll be able to keep my balance.

June 12

Day four of working in the boutique. Surprisingly, I seem to be getting it. I can write up a purchase, run the credit card, wrap the purchase in tissue, and bag it without even blinking now. The only thing I don't get is Vivian. I doubt that anyone can figure out that woman. Sometimes I wonder if she's doing drugs. Or maybe she's bipolar or has some sort of personality disorder. Because occasionally she's actually rather nice. Although, come to think of it, it's nice like a spider enticing you into her web. Just when you begin to trust her, the fangs come out, and she goes into her mean mode. It's best to keep a low profile around this woman.

But from observing Em, I'm learning some clever ways to avoid the wrath of Vivian. (1) Appear to be busy, even if it means making a mess of something (when Vivian is *not* looking) just so you can clean it up; (2) engage a client by complimenting her on something she's wearing or her hair, and then keep chatting with her until Vivian moves on; and (3) initiate a conversation with Vivian by telling her about some big purchase that was made while she was out, or mention someone famous who stepped in and complimented the shop—even if you have to make it up (not the purchase, but the celebrity). See, I'm learning fast. Still, I feel more like a hypocrite than ever.

But here's the good news. I've earned $240 by now. I can't believe it! Oh, sure, I don't get paid until Friday, but I'm keeping careful track of my hours, and by Friday I should have made a total of $360. I realize that's not much by some people's standards, but for a girl who has to buy her own groceries, it's pretty good. I plan to start seriously saving now. My goal is to have enough money put aside by my sixteenth birthday (December 12) to show that I can live on my own. The beginning of my emancipation proclamation.

June 14

Payday! Okay, the thrill quickly evaporated when I saw that my check wasn't $360, like I'd anticipated. Fortunately, Em explained the concept of deductions. It seems that Uncle Sam needs my money—probably to do stupid things like buy guns and tanks. And then there are things like Social Security, like that will even exist by the time I need it, and workmen's comp, whatever that is. Anyway, it was a bit disheartening to realize that, unlike baby-sitting, you don't actually make what you feel you earned. And minimum wage is just what it sounds like. Minimal. How could a person survive on it?

"They can't," Em explained as she steamed a blouse.

I know now that Em lives with three roommates, including her boyfriend, Vic. She started college but dropped out due to lack of interest combined with a lack of funds. But she, unlike me, has a genuine interest in the fashion industry, and that's why she subjects herself to Vivian. Well, that and to pay the bills. She also informed me that after two years in this shop and after threatening to leave, she finally was put on commission, meaning she gets a tiny percentage of what she sells. "It helps out," she told me.

I was tempted to tell Em a little more about myself and my emancipation plan, but I'm afraid to disclose too much. Thanks to Shannon and probably Vivian as well now, I have a bit of paranoia. I will play my cards close to my chest.

"Do you think I can get on commission too?" I asked eagerly. I was considering how I'd sold nearly a thousand dollars' worth of clothes just that morning. Even a 5 percent cut would equal fifty bucks—not exactly chump change for a girl in my shoes (which were hurting my feet as usual).

"You can ask…" But even as Em said this, I could tell she was doubtful.

"Maybe after a while..."

During my lunch break I walked to the bank, the very same branch where Dad took me to open my own savings account about ten years ago. Sure, that account has only had about thirty dollars in it for the past several years, but that's changing now. I considered hiding my cash in the house, but that's backfired on me before. If Shannon's in dire need of chemicals, it's like she can actually sniff out money. Oh, I've been more fortunate since creating my attic getaway, but I don't think I can be too careful when it comes to my mom.

My plan is to deposit $450 of every two-week paycheck for a total of $900 a month. That doesn't leave me with much money for living expenses, but as long as Dad doesn't get too far behind on child support, I should be just fine. Better than ever in fact. Since my first paycheck isn't very big, I only put in $150. But it's a start. According to my calculations (and I wonder if I should get some homeschool math credit for all this), I'll have more than $5,500 by my birthday. Even more if I can deposit some money from Dad's child-support payments.

"How much rent do you have to pay per month?" I asked Em this afternoon.

"Two hundred and fifty dollars," she told me as she held up a silky dress and looked in the mirror.

"That's not much," I said hopefully.

"Well, that's because Vic pays for part of my rent. You know, since he makes more money than I do."

"Yeah, right..."

"I think I'm going to have to get this." She hung the dress on the "hold" rack.

I tried not to look shocked as I glanced at the price tag. I've learned by now, first from Shannon and then from working here, that nothing is too expensive when it comes to style. Yeah, right. Even so, I couldn't control myself, and knowing that Vivian was not in the building, I had to ask. "How can you afford that?" I held up the tag. "That's more than your rent."

Em just laughed. "It's Tadashi," she said, as if that explained it all.

"I know, but still."

"And you know we have an employee discount, silly."

I blinked. "Yeah, like 20 percent. That's still about the same amount as you pay for a month's rent."

"Yes, but I can't wear rent, now can I? And Vic is taking me to a corporate dinner where appearances are every-thing." She looked slightly perplexed. "The real question is shoes."

"Shoes?"

"Yes. I'm not sure I have the right ones for this dress."

"What's wrong with the ones you're wearing?"

She laughed again. "Puhleeze."

Just then the bell on the door tinkled, and I was relieved to go help a customer who hopefully could actually afford the clothes in here. In my opinion, a girl should never pay more than her rent for a dress she will probably wear only once. But what do I know?

As it turned out, the customers were teen girls about my age. And remembering Vivian's wrath when the "dumpy redhead" stole the Fendi sandals, I was not letting these girls out of my sight either. They weren't the same group as the shoplifters, and these girls looked like they could easily afford to shop here. Although I've only been observing fashion for a week or so, I recognized that they were wearing some pretty expensive threads. In fact these girls looked a lot like ones on *The O.C.* Yes, I'll admit I used to watch that show back in middle school. Mostly due to peer pressure. I wouldn't be caught dead watching anything like that now. I don't care much for television in general. Unless it's what I consider educational.

"I can't believe Leo invited Capri to the party tomorrow night," said a thin brunette as she held up a pale blue gauzy blouse. "I mean, after the way she treated Ambrose last week, you'd think that Leo wouldn't want to subject his best friend to her anymore."

"I agree completely," said the blonde with her. "Seriously, Capri, of all people, really deserves to be shunned right now."

The brunette laughed. "Just don't let your brother hear you saying that. I think Leo's still got a crush on her."

"I've been keeping my thoughts to myself." The blonde nodded approval now. "You really should try that blouse on, Jenna."

The brunette held it up in front of her friend. "No, I think it's more you than me, Miranda."

Just then the blonde turned and stared at me like she thought I was eavesdropping or something.

"Uh, can I help you guys find anything?" I offered quickly, feeling less than invisible, not to mention intrusive. The truth was, I had been eavesdropping. I don't even know why. Maybe I just miss talking to girls my own age.

"You work here?" demanded the brunette in a challenging way.

I nodded. "That's why I asked if you needed help." Then I smiled at the blonde. "I think your friend is right. That top would look fantastic on you. It really goes with your eyes."

Now the blonde smiled slightly. "Really?"

"Yeah," her friend said, "it does."

And for a few minutes it was like these two girls, Jenna and Miranda, were actually my friends. Okay, not really. Maybe I was just imagining or pretending, but as I helped them pick out some things for Saturday night's party, I almost felt like I was one of them, like I was going to the party too. They finished shopping, and I rang them up on their credit cards, which I assume are paid by their parents. Then they thanked me for helping them and happily told me good-bye, and I felt sorry to see them go. That's when I realized just how pathetic and lame I really am.

And now it's Friday night, and I am home alone. Shannon swore to me that she was only going out for a few hours. But I don't expect to see her for a few days. It occurs to me that I could start up some kind of social life for myself…but I wonder who that would be with. Despite being drawn in with Miranda and Jenna today, I usually feel out of place with people my own age. Quite honestly, I get bored with their shallow values. And it's awkward hanging with people who are older, because they usually act weird when they discover how young I am. Maybe I'm destined to be a misfit forever.

Okay, now I'm trying to come up with a green tip, and yet I feel like a hypocrite because I still can't believe I'm being paid to sell overpriced clothes. That feels so wrong in so many ways. And yet a girl has to make a living. But that gives me a green tip idea. Because although I've been sneaking things from Shannon's closet lately (my own form of recycling), my favorite way to shop for fashions is at the secondhand store—and that is very green.

Maya's Green Tip of the Day

Call them "thrift" or "vintage" or "gently used," second-hand clothes are a great way to help our environment. And most things you find in thrift shops are good for another go-round. Look for pieces that are barely worn (like my favorite OshKosh overalls). But you can also find items with character and history (like my tie-dyed sundress from the sixties). Not only is shopping second-hand environmentally friendly, but it also brings out a person's creativity. Just think, while you're putting together some great one-of-a-kind outfits, you're also protecting the environment in two ways. You're preventing more junk from piling up in landfills, and you're preserving precious natural resources.

Seven

June 20

It's my day off, and I'm as bored as a gourd. Speaking of gourds, my garden is coming along nicely. I harvested numerous things, including cucumbers, tomatoes, lettuce, basil, and some baby carrots. I spent a couple of pleasant hours just weeding and watering and working on my compost this morning before it got too hot. It's also wise to water in the morning, because that's the best way to conserve water (it doesn't evaporate so quickly), and the plants seem to like it better too. I guess I should make a green tip about that someday.

Anyway, to my complete surprise, Shannon actually made it home last night. Although I'm certain she was totally wasted because I heard her stumbling up the stairs on her way to her room. I considered offering some help but figured it served her right if she fell and broke her leg. Plus that might keep her at home. She eventually made it up, and when her bedroom door slammed, I went back to sleep. As usual, she's sleeping in. And I sort of enjoy having the house to myself in the mornings.

I felt at loose ends. I straightened up the kitchen some and even sat and watched some public television, about the only worthwhile thing we get these days since Shannon hasn't paid the cable bill in months. Not that I care. But the constant phone calls do bug me. I'm actually surprised that our land-line is still working. I don't think Shannon has paid that lately either. But most of our calls are from grumpy collections peo-ple, and we just let them go straight to the machine. Occa-sionally someone will come to the door, but Shannon has made it clear that I'm not to answer the door unless we know the person. So mostly I ignore that too.

But this morning when someone knocked, I took a peek at the security monitor—a system my dad had set up for us back when he was worried about stalkers. Anyway, I was only looking out of curiosity...and boredom, I sup-pose. But the guy standing there was probably from a col-lection agency, so no way was I opening the door. Yet, as I stood there looking at the camera, I found myself wishing it were one of my old friends just stopping by to say *hey*. That used to happen. But not anymore. And then I actually considered calling up my old best friend, Ashlee. But I know she's so moved on by now. She probably wouldn't even remember who I am. Sometimes I have difficulty re-membering myself.

Finally, around noon, Shannon crawled out. I could tell by her puffy face and bloodshot eyes that she'd been drinking. But she seemed slightly proud of herself for finding her way home. And she was grouchy.

"Where's the coffee?" she demanded.

"I didn't make any." I filled a water bottle, getting ready to make a quick exit.

"Why not?"

"I wanted tea." I made my way to the door.

"Are you going to work now?" She obviously hadn't really looked at me since my overalls, T-shirt, and flip-flops should've given the answer.

"No."

"Hey, baby," she said in her I-need-something voice, "do you have any money?"

"Not really," I lied.

She scowled. "Nothing?"

"A few bucks."

"Don't they pay you at that chichi shop?"

I just shrugged. "I can loan you a few bucks until Dad's check gets here, Shannon." Loan, yeah right. Like she'll ever pay me back.

"Yeah, that'd be good."

So I went and got into my secret cash stash and pulled out a twenty. A twenty I will never see again. Okay, maybe Shannon is my way of giving to charity. Whatever.

Then I hopped on my bike and rode over to Beverly Gardens Park. It's not a big park, but I remember Dad bringing me here as a little girl...and for that reason I still like to come here sometimes. Today I'm sitting by the lily pond, doodling and writing in my journal. I know I must look lonely. I stopped by the *Hunter and Hounds* statue. It's kind of a memorial to a soldier in World War I. But as I look at the dogs, I think maybe that's what I need. A dog to keep me company. Oh sure, Shannon would have a fit. Other times when I've raised the dog subject, she's always said that she couldn't afford to keep a dog. Well, the truth is, she can't afford to keep a daughter either. If I got a dog, it would be completely mine. And I would take care of everything it needed. Still, I'm not sure how much that would cost. I've heard that vet bills can be expensive, and I'm not sure how I'd feel about buying dog food since it's primarily meat. I guess I might have to think about that.

Mostly I think I'd like a friend. But not just any friend. I've had friends in the past who have hurt me. I think the next time I make friends, serious friends, I'll be very selective. Okay, that makes me laugh. Well, almost. I mean, here I am sitting by myself in a park where only old people walk, and I am feeling lonely and acting like I can be so choosy about a friend. Maybe I need to lower my standards. After all, I certainly lowered them when it came to employment. If you ask me, selling costly designer clothes is only a notch above selling red meat. Who woulda thunk?

June 25

I keep hoping that Vivian's mood swings will even out, but I'm beginning to think that, like Shannon, she is beyond hope. I'm fairly certain that she is beyond reason. I cannot understand how Em has lasted so long. Two years? I've only been here a little over two weeks, and I want to run the other direction every time Vivian opens her mouth.

"How long do you think you'll work here?" I asked Em earlier today. It was safe to talk since Vivian had just left to meet some friends for lunch. I'm surprised that she actually has friends, or maybe she's making that part up. Maybe she's actually sitting by herself at a corner table and reading the paper as she nibbles on a Caesar salad.

"I don't know..." Even though she was standing behind the counter, I could tell she was slipping off her shoes. Hopefully the video camera wasn't catching this. Although I was sure Em had figured out how to avoid the cameras. I even had a suspicion that she might occasionally steal things, since I saw her carrying a pair of jeans over to a part of the shop that made no sense...except that it's kind of a dead spot when it comes to the video camera. She set the jeans, which happened to be her size, at the bottom of a rack of oversize bags, and later that same day I noticed they had disappeared. Naturally, I would never mention this to anyone.

"Do you have any specific career plans?" I asked her as I made myself look busy straightening a rack of dresses (for the sake of the cameras). "I mean, on down the line." Em is twenty-two, and although she dropped out of college, I'd think she'd try to figure a way to complete her education.

"I used to think I wanted to go to design school." She leaned her elbows on the counter—another huge no-no when Vivian is around. "But it's a pretty competitive field. I'm not so sure now."

"But if you really loved it…," I tried, hoping to keep her talking. I can't explain why, but I am so starved for friendship…it's like I even imagine myself becoming friends with Em.

"Vic and I used to love doing music," she said dreamily.

"You're a musician?"

"Not really. I mean, I can sing okay. And Vic is really brilliant on guitar. We used to have a band."

"What kind of music?"

"Jazz mostly. Cool jazz. And we were doing pretty well at picking up gigs, just local bars and stuff. But it was fun."

"Why'd you stop?"

"It wasn't paying the bills. Vic took a real job…and then life got busy."

"It's not easy being a musician."

She nodded. "I know."

I was pretty sure Em didn't know about my dad's career. Not that I want her to know, but I can usually tell if people know or not, especially if they are into music. Anyway,

I had a feeling Vivian hadn't mentioned it to her. She probably didn't want Em to treat me differently or something. I
was tempted to bring it up just then, to keep the conversation rolling. But it seemed a little pathetic. Sort of like trying to buy a friendship—like "do you like me now that you
know my dad is kind of famous?" So I didn't say anything.
And it was just as well since customers came in about that
time.

June 28

Today is payday again. And I must say, I have mixed feelings
about this day. On one hand, I'm totally stoked when Vivian
hands me that white envelope with my check in it. On the
other hand, I'm not sure how much of her guilt tripping I
can take.

I thank her as I finger the long, thin envelope, suppressing the desire to rip it open.

She frowns slightly. "You know, I'm not used to employees who don't make purchases in my shop, Maya. It hardly
seems right."

I want to point out that I cannot afford to purchase even
a pair of socks from this ridiculously expensive store, but I
bite my tongue and just nod in a way I hope looks a tiny bit
sympathetic.

Then Vivian hands Em her paycheck, along with a catty
smile. "Some employees have been known to take home

only a few dollars on payday...but at least their wardrobes improve."

I look down at my outfit and realize that it's not quite as chic as some I've worn in the past. I have on an aqua Chloé T-shirt topped with a little black vest from the thrift shop. I'm also wearing a pair of khaki capri pants using an old men's tie as a belt, and on my feet I have those Prada slides I've already worn several times recently. And they are finally starting to feel slightly broken in. I might've done better with my clothes except that Shannon has been home for most of the week. A rarity that I should appreciate, but it does put a hitch in my fashion plans when I can't go closet shopping. Apparently Vivian has noticed. Still, I remain mute. What you don't say won't hurt you.

Then on my lunch break, I go to the bank and make an even larger deposit into my savings. It feels so good to see the amount getting bigger. It gives me hope. I walk back to work feeling slightly lighthearted. Well, until I have to stop and put on my less-than-comfortable "work" shoes. Naturally, that brings me back to reality. But as I go into the back room to stow my purse, Vivian is waiting in the shadows, like a tiger about to pounce. I actually hold my breath as I walk past her.

"Someone's been stealing from me," she announces as I close the door to my locker. A locker that I'm fairly certain she also has a key to. Not that I care. I don't have anything to hide.

"Shoplifters?"

She glares at me, then shakes her head. "No, Maya, this is an inside job."

"An inside job?"

She nods in a sly way. Her eyes look like slits behind today's red-rimmed glasses, and she stares at me like I'm the one to blame here. And even though I am not the slightest bit guilty, I almost begin to feel I have done something wrong. *This is ridiculous.*

"Well, don't look at me," I say in a tone I mean to sound light but might sound defensive.

"I *am* looking at you."

"Why?"

"Why?" She repeats the word slowly as if she's chewing on it, like a cat with a morsel of raw meat in her mouth.

I wait without speaking.

"Well, I don't think it's Em."

"And?" I return her stare now. *I can play this game too.*

"*And* that leaves you, Maya."

I simply shrug at this accusation. "Well, you can think whatever you like, Vivian. But I haven't stolen as much as a paper clip from you."

She makes a noise that sounds like *harrumph,* then walks into her office, where I'm sure she'll carefully go over her precious videotapes. Well, fine. Let her. Maybe she'll find the culprit. And maybe I was right about Em. Maybe she did take those Diesel jeans after all.

I tell myself to just shrug it off. The same way I might shrug off Shannon. Vivian will figure out I'm innocent. But even so, I feel angry and indignant as I return to work. As if it's not bad enough that I've compromised my personal values to work here, now I'm suspected of thievery. I walk through the shop looking for something to do, something to distract me from fuming at Vivian and her stupid accusations. Then I notice Em standing behind the counter. She smiles at me like nothing's wrong and announces she's going to lunch.

I try to act natural as I smile back at her, but I feel resentful that Em might be responsible for this. Could she have somehow insinuated that I stole the merchandise? But why would she do it? Perhaps to draw attention from herself? But that's so wrong. So low. And to think I was trying to be friendly with her. I should've known better.

Fortunately some customers come in, a very well-dressed couple who are probably my mom's age, and I am distracted with trying to help them. And I'm surprised at how friendly they are. But then I've seen the woman here before, just a few days ago. Finally the woman says something odd to the man.

"See, what did I tell you about her?"

Now I'm not sure how to respond...or whether to, so I sort of step back, giving them their space. The woman opens her purse, a very expensive Ralph Lauren bag (I can tell by the initials in the lining), and she removes a card and hands it to me.

"If you're ever looking for work," she says quietly, as if she doesn't wish to be overheard, "you just give me a call."

I blink and try not to look too shocked. "Thank you."

She smiles, and the man nods, and then they leave. After they're gone, I head over to the dead spot and read the card. The woman is the manager of the Ralph Lauren shop—a shop that is much nicer than this one. So I'm standing here, thinking that it's flattering and in some ways tempting, when Vivian comes out and insists on knowing what I am doing.

I tuck the card into my vest pocket and look evenly at her. "I'm actually just standing here."

"Why here?"

"Why not?"

"Hold out your hands."

So I put my hands up, palms forward, as if she's holding a gun on me.

"Empty your pockets."

"My pockets?" I frown at her.

"Yes. Your pockets. Step over to the counter and empty them, Maya."

I go over by the cash register and empty my pockets. This is a little embarrassing because I have, among other things, a used tissue, a dog-eared stick of clove gum, and my worry stone. Finally I set the business card down as well.

She examines the contents of my pockets and even picks up the stone. "What's this?"

"A worry stone," I say with a sigh, thinking I could've used it right then.

"And this?" She holds up the business card.

"Someone gave it to me."

She scowls now. "And you have nothing else in your pockets?"

"Do you want to frisk me?"

She goes back to where I was standing in the dead spot and carefully searches through the bags to see if I've tucked something back there. Finally she seems to give up. But when she returns, she's still looking at me in an accusatory way. "Why were you standing over there, Maya?"

I pick up the business card again. "I was slipping this into my pocket."

"Why?"

"Because those people who were just in here offered me a job at their store." I stand up straighter now. "And, as a matter of fact, I think I will take them up on it. I quit."

She actually sputters at this. But ignoring her, I go to the back room, pick up my purse, and walk out. Then I march over to the Ralph Lauren shop, where I show the first employee I see the business card, and the next thing I know, I'm sitting in a very nice office and explaining to that nice woman, who

tells me to call her by her first name, what happened with
Viv.

"Oh, I hope we didn't get you fired," Diane says.

"No, but my boss confronted me just now. She saw the
card and wanted to know how I got it. So I told her the truth.
She wasn't very pleased, but to be honest, she's not the easiest person to work for either."

"So we've heard."

And suddenly I am signing a tax form and explaining
about my age and the work permit.

"Don't worry about that," Diane says. "The reason you
caught my eye is because you look exactly like one of Ralph's
favorite models, and I thought we just had to get you in our
shop."

"Oh…"

"You'll be working in sales, but I hope we can entice
you to wear some of the clothing as well. Kind of a walking
advertisement."

I shrug. "Sure, that'd be fine."

"Naturally, we'll take the ordinary precautions so that
none of the garments are damaged. And if you wish to purchase any, you'll get a nice discount."

Okay, I decide to lay my cards on the table this time. "The
truth is, I'm working because I really need the money. I probably won't be spending much, if any, of it on clothing."

"I understand." And then she smiles in a way that makes me think perhaps she really does understand. After that, a woman named Betsy puts together a work schedule for me that starts on Monday.

So it was that I began the day employed in one place and ended it employed in another. Go figure.

Maya's Green Tip for the Day

"Dry clean only." Hey, did you know that 95 percent of dry cleaners use a toxic chemical called perc (per-chloroethylene) that's bad not only for the planet but also for the workers who do the cleaning? And another thing most people don't know is that many clothes with labels that say "Dry clean only" can be safely cleaned at home. Many delicate items can be hand-washed with luke-warm water and shampoo. Yes, shampoo. It's very gen-tle. Another alternative is to spot-clean a garment (washcloth and a little soapy water) and then hang it in the sun to dry. The sun is a great natural disinfectant and cleaner.

Eight

July 1

It's odd how I don't worry about Shannon so much anymore. I think it's partially due to the fact that I'm distracted trying to earn a living, or maybe I'm just suppressing my real feelings. Anyway, Shannon took off Friday night, and it's been three days since I've seen her. I figure she's (1) out on another binge, (2) locked up in jail, or (3) dead. I know that sounds terrible, but after so many nights of fretting over her, I have developed my own survival tactics. I would include "in the hospital" on my list, but I assume someone would call me if that were the case. Okay, I really hope she's not dead. Or even locked up. But it aggravates me to think she's out bingeing again or partying. Seriously, someone as old as Shannon should know better. Shouldn't she?

But I think that's part of the problem too. It's like she's stuck in the mind-set of a twenty-year-old. Like she thinks she's a Lindsay Lohan or Paris Hilton or even a Britney Spears. I wonder how those girls will act when they're Shannon's age. Will they ever grow up? Or are some people just destined to be messed up for their entire lives? And why is that anyway? Well, enough of psychoanalyzing my mom. Talk about a formula for an instant headache.

Today was my first day working for Ralph. (Okay, Ralph Lauren wasn't actually there, although I've heard he does come in occasionally.) Anyway, I have to say that it was a little bit better than working for Vivian. Well, other than the part about selling overpriced clothes to people who have too much time and money on their hands.

And there is still that thing with some employees...like there's this hierarchy in the workplace. Or perhaps some consider the new girl to be a threat, which seems perfectly ridiculous.

After the manager of the women's department, a tall, older woman named Monica, gave me the general tour, she invited me to wear one of Ralph's latest designs. She held up a dark blue knit dress that didn't actually seem too spectacular, although I liked it for that very reason. In a way it seemed rather ordinary and down to earth. Sort of like me. Well, other than the staggering price tag.

"These just came in," she explained. "From the fall collection."

"Nice." I nodded my approval.

"We like to show off the new lines," she continued as she led me to an employee-only dressing room in the back of the store. "You'll need this, of course." She handed me a package of what I at first assumed was Kotex.

"What?" I tried not to look shocked. I mean, I wasn't planning on getting my period for at least two weeks.

"Disposable perspiration pads to protect the garment," she explained as she picked up a silver can of what looked like industrial-strength antiperspirant. "And you'll need this too." The can had been on a small shelf that also held hair spray and several other primping products.

I tried not to look too disgusted as I examined the can, but there was no way I would put that stuff on my armpits or anywhere else on my body for that matter.

"And what size shoe do you wear?"

"Nine."

"I'll be back shortly." She pointed to a package of dark blue stockings. "Those go with the dress. And I'll bring some accessories along with the shoes."

I soon figured out that the perspiration pads had an adhesive strip that could adhere to the underarms of the dress. But I had to *just say no* to that scary-looking antiperspirant. I felt certain it was loaded with all kinds of cancer-causing chemicals.

By the time I was dressed, Monica returned with shoes, a wide leather belt, and some other accessories. She helped me with these, then stepped back and smiled. "Ralph would be proud."

"Thanks."

"You could model, you know."

I sort of shrugged.

"Really, you have the right look."

"Uh, thanks." I suddenly felt totally self-conscious, like, *What am I doing here? How did I end up like this?* Then I reminded myself it was simply a temporary and desperate measure. The first step of my emancipation plan. *Just bite the bullet and collect the paycheck.*

"You really should consider it, Maya. Models make good money."

I did consider that as I went back into the shop in search of the young brunette I'd met earlier. Her name was Britt, and she was supposed to train me. But as soon as I found her, she gave me one of those looks. It's hard to explain and is probably more a feeling than anything else. But I noticed that her eyes narrowed ever so slightly, and I could tell that something about me was not fully meeting her approval.

"I'm ready to be trained," I announced, acting oblivious to the vibes I was receiving.

"I can't believe they're letting you wear *that* on your first day."

"Is there something wrong with it?"

"No...it's just that you're new. I'd think they'd want to break you in a bit first."

"Oh...well, if you're worried that I might take off with this dress, you don't need to be. I'm not a thief."

"That's not it," she said quickly. "I'm just surprised to see you wearing it. That line arrived only last week. It's barely on the racks."

I forced a smile and then shrugged. "Hey, I just follow orders."

Britt let out an exasperated sigh. Then she began walking me through the paces, explaining what I was supposed to do and how I was supposed to do it as if it were very complicated, which seems a little ridiculous. Selling clothes isn't exactly brain surgery or rocket science.

Anyway, it seems my job is mostly to assist the customers in finding what they're looking for, or not looking for, in the shop. Consequently, I must learn where everything is. I must know how to present items in a way that makes a customer feel she cannot live without them. I must compliment her and show her accessories, and I must make the sale. Then, when it comes to the customer actually purchasing merchandise, I pass her along to the cashier but in such a way that she doesn't feel like I've passed her on. She must feel as if we are all there to serve her. Her slightest wish is our greatest command.

"We treat the customer like an honored guest," Britt explained. "We cater to whatever she wants. Perhaps she wants us to watch her kids while she tries something on. Or to give her husband an espresso while he waits. Or simply to tell her how absolutely fantastic she looks in an outfit."

I nodded. "That doesn't sound too difficult."

Britt sort of laughed. "Maybe it doesn't sound too difficult right now, but some customers, rather *guests*,...well, they can be trying. Just don't let it show. You're here to make them happy. Consider yourself part of the hospitality industry."

I also got to consider myself a clothes rack. As it turned out, certain customers wouldn't try on an outfit without seeing it on a model first. That's where I came in. I tried on about five different outfits before the day was over. But I guess that helped pass the time.

July 6

The store was busy today. Okay, that doesn't mean the aisles were filled with people. It means we might've had more than three customers in our department at the same time. Naturally, there were a few more spread out through the store. I am helping an older woman with a cable-knit cotton cardigan sweater "for cool nights on the water" when I hear someone say, "Maya Stark?"

I look up to see an attractive woman about my mom's age smiling at me. She is obviously a customer and being helped by Britt, but she's also vaguely familiar.

"Don't you remember me, Maya?"

I blink at her and attempt a smile.

"You don't, do you?"

"Perhaps you'd like Maya to help you," Britt says in a polite tone. She steps over to my customer, giving me a glance that suggests we swap customers, rather *guests*.

"If you'll excuse me," I say to the older woman, although she doesn't look the least bit pleased by our switcheroo, "Britt can help you with this."

"I'm sorry," says the woman with the vaguely familiar face. "But I'm an old friend of Maya's father. You know the famous Nick Stark."

Now the older woman turns and smiles at me. "You're Nick Stark's daughter?"

I swallow and nod. So far I had managed to keep this little tidbit to myself.

The older woman grabs me by the elbow. "I simply adore Nick Stark. My daughter got us tickets to his concert in Philadelphia. I plan to see him when I fly out there in August."

"So you'll forgive me for stealing her now, won't you?" says the other woman. "I'm a friend of the family, and I'm just dying to hear how they're all doing these days."

The older woman doesn't look quite ready to forgive the intruder, but at least she doesn't make a scene as the woman pulls me away.

"I'll get her next time." The older woman shakes her finger in the air.

I smile at her. "Absolutely!"

Then I follow the "friend of the family" over to a quiet corner of the store, trying to recall who she is. Her voice actually sounds familiar.

"I'm Myrna Fallows," she tells me with enthusiasm.

"Myrna?" I nod as realization sinks in. "I didn't recognize you." Myrna had been my dad's publicist when I was very little. Back when he still needed a publicist. Sometimes he would take me to a mall appearance or a restaurant opening, and Myrna would keep me entertained until he was finished. I used to really like her. "It's been so long since I've seen you."

Her eyes light up. "Yes. Remember now?"

"How are you doing?"

"I was about to ask you the same thing, Maya. It's been ages. And look at you now, so grown-up."

"How did you know it was me?"

"Well, I'll admit that a certain pretty young woman caught my eye when I came in here. And then I noticed your nametag, and I put two and two together." She peers into my face. "Those eyes, girl. No one has eyes quite like those."

"Besides my dad, you mean."

She winks at me. "Don't we know it. My, you've grown into a beautiful girl, Maya. How old are you now?"

"Just fifteen," I say quietly.

She smiles in a knowing sort of way. "Look, sweetheart, I came in here for a black blazer." She pats her midsection.

"Something sophisticated and slimming. I'm going to New York on Monday, and it seems that everyone there still thinks that black is the new black."

I lead her over to a rack and pull out a blazer that seems to fit her description. "How about this?"

She examines it, then nods, whispering to me her size. I search until I find a twelve as well as a ten and a fourteen, since you never know, and I lead her back to the dressing room.

"It's perfect," she says from behind the dressing room door. Then she comes out and hands it to me. "I'll take it."

As I walk her to the cashier, she asks me if I have plans for lunch.

"Besides putting my feet up?" I say quietly.

"Let me take you to lunch, Maya." She has her cell phone out. "I'll call and see if I can get us a table right away."

So I agree and tell her when my lunch break is, and she tells me where to meet her. Of course, this means another quick change since I'm not allowed to wear store clothing off the premises. But the thought of getting out for some fresh air makes it seem worth the trouble.

There aren't too many restaurants around Rodeo Drive. I think it's because retail shops make more money. As a result, the restaurants around here are pretty spendy, and I haven't been going to them much since times have gotten hard at home. I suspect that Shannon still meets friends occasionally. Not while she's bingeing like she's been doing lately. Not only is she too broke, but her use of drugs and alcohol take a toll on her appearance, and she doesn't like being seen by certain people when she looks like that. After all, she has an image to keep up.

"Maya, Maya," says Myrna when I finally join her, "it is so good to see you again. And I've been following Nick's comeback. Very impressive." She shakes her head. "I wish I'd been available to represent him again."

"I'm sure he wishes the same thing."

"But I'm sure Jess Jordan is doing a great job. She's good."

I nod, pretending like I really keep up on this. To be honest, my head is spinning. I can't believe I'm having lunch in this restaurant with Dad's old publicist. It feels kind of surreal.

"How is your mom?" she asks in a tentative way. Like she knows or maybe just suspects the answer.

I kind of shrug. "Oh, she's…well, you know…"

Myrna nods. "Yes, I do kind of know. And I've heard rumors."

"Rumors?" Now I feel nervous. *What are people saying?*

"You know, Maya, the same old same-old."

Suddenly, and despite how crazy it seems, I feel the need to defend Shannon. "She had been doing better. But then she heard that her sister had died. And she hadn't been in touch with her for ages. I think it kind of derailed her."

"Does your dad know?"

"Sort of...well, not exactly. I mean, I don't want to distract him."

Myrna puts on what seems a forced smile. "And you are working."

"Yeah. I thought it might be fun."

Myrna doesn't look convinced. "Fun?"

I give her a half smile. "Okay, I need the money."

"Addictions can be costly...in many ways."

"I know."

Myrna reaches across the table and takes my chin in her hand, tilting my head this way and that. "You could model, Maya."

I jerk my head away from her hands.

"I have connections. I could set up some—"

"I don't think I'd like that."

"But there's money to be—"

"So I've heard."

She smiles. "I'm sorry. Listen to me, always the opportunist. But should you change your mind, you just get in touch."

"It's just that I'm really not into all that. I don't like being in the limelight. And fashion is..." I hold up my hands and roll my eyes.

"Stupid?" She chuckles.

"Exactly. If I could do whatever I wanted, I'd join Greenpeace and protect endangered marine life."

"I understand." She pats my hand, and I get the feeling she really does understand. And suddenly I consider telling her everything. I consider confessing about my emancipation plan, about how I'm hiding my money from Shannon. My fears, my loneliness, my pathetic excuse of homeschooling—everything. But I don't. I can't.

Instead we move on to more chitchat, and we eat what turns out to be a pretty good lunch. Fortunately there's a vegan entrée on the menu. Finally, my break is nearly over, and I have to run.

"Thanks for everything," I tell her as I stand.

"Take my card." She pushes an ivory card across the table. "And call me, Maya, if you need anything. Okay?"

I thank her again, then I slip her card into a pocket of my bag. I head back to the store, and the whole time I'm wondering, *Can I trust her? Can I?* I so need a friend. Even if it's an older friend. Just someone—someone I can trust... and talk to.

Now that I'm home, I've stashed Myrna's card in my secret place, along with my cash and savings account card. Just in case.

Maya's Green Tip for the Day

Did you know that public transportation saves 1.5 billion gallons of gas each year? And did you know that more that 200 million commuting vehicles (many with only one person inside) log up to nearly two trillion miles on our roads each year—and contribute about 50 percent of our air pollution (more in big cities)? Anyway, here's my point. Why not see if there's a form of public transportation next time you want to go to the mall? Or just do the earth a favor and ride your bike!

July 31

This has been the longest month of my life. Working full-time is not easy. The good news is that I've been earning lots of money. And most of it is going straight into the bank. I can't believe how good it feels to make a deposit. Then I just read the numbers on my passbook and get this fantastic rush. I wonder if saving money could become an addiction.

Speaking of addictions, the other good news is that Shannon has actually started an outpatient rehab treatment program that my dad is financing. Kim had urged me to e-mail him about my concerns, and I finally took her advice. I told him almost everything. Oh, not about my emancipation plan, but I did tell him that our finances were a mess and that Shannon was out of control. He called her, and they had a long talk. I eavesdropped for a while. Just long enough to hear Shannon finally calm down and listen. I think he pressured her some. My guess is he threatened to stop sending money or something to that effect. Anyway, it got her attention, and for the past two weeks she has been going in for counseling sessions and group meetings. Also, as far as I can tell, she has stayed clean. At least she hasn't gone AWOL.

The hard part about Shannon staying clean is that she's grouchier than ever. I'm thankful to have a job to get me out of the house. Yet I have a hard time believing that this treatment program is really going to change things for us. It's like I keep expecting it to go sideways again. And every time I come home from work, I hold my breath. I expect to find her gone—off bingeing again. Then I'm surprised to discover she's still here. And sure, I'm glad she's here, but at the same time, I'm afraid I'll get my hopes up and then she'll blow it and it'll hurt more than ever.

The other hard part about Shannon staying clean and sober is that she hardly leaves the house now. And when she's home like this, she makes messes that she doesn't clean up. I try to ignore them, but sometimes I get fed up. Even so, it would be useless to confront her. That would probably just make her mad enough to stomp out and do something stupid. So sometimes I clean up the messes. But other times I'm just too tired, so I go to my room and pretend like I haven't noticed.

August 10

Today when I got home from work, Shannon was gone. If it wasn't a Saturday, I might assume she'd gone to a meeting. But so far her appointments and meetings have been during

the week. And it's after ten now. I tried her cell phone a couple of hours ago, knowing full well that she usually turns it off
if she's doing something she shouldn't be doing. It was
off...and it's still off now. I have a bad feeling. I knew this
would happen. I knew she wasn't really going to stay clean.
And as I think this, I wonder if I'm wrong. Maybe she's not
out getting high. Finally I just can't think about it anymore.
Not without going crazy. I wish I had someone I could call.

I consider calling Dad, but I'm pretty sure he's got a
concert since it's Saturday. Plus it's after midnight on the
East Coast, and I think that's where he is right now. I consider e-mailing Kim, but I hate to bug her. And the last time
I e-mailed her it was to say that things were going well. Now
it feels like a failure to admit they are not going so well. I
think I'll put an old video in and watch it. Maybe Shannon
will come home after all.

August 11

Shannon came home. But not until this morning. When I
confronted her about her missing act, asking how it fit into
her rehab program, she swore she had not done any drugs.
But I could tell she'd been drinking and said as much.

"You're not my mommy, Maya," she told me angrily.

"No, but sometimes it feels like I am. Have you ever considered picking up the phone and letting someone know
where you are?"

"Quit being such a worrywart." She poured herself a mug of coffee, then dumped about half a cup of sugar into it.

"Why don't you quit partying all night?" I tossed back as she walked away.

"Just because I'm doing rehab doesn't mean I'm not supposed to have a social life."

"Going out on Saturday and coming home wasted on Sunday is not a social life."

"Coming from you, the expert?" Shannon was heading toward the stairs now. "Get a life, daughter dear."

I couldn't think of a retort to this because what she said was true. Mean but true. My social life is nonexistent. Still, I'd rather have no social life than live like Shannon does. And although I didn't say it, I wanted to point out that going out drinking one night could easily lead to doing drugs the next.

August 16

Turns out I was right. Or at least I think I was right. Shannon took off again on Wednesday, and now it's Friday, and she's still gone. It doesn't take a genius to figure it out. I haven't even tried to call her. Her phone will be off.

Once again I longed for someone to talk to about this. But who? Then as I was putting my savings passbook away, feeling that cool rush from having made another deposit today,

I noticed Myrna's business card. So I tucked my precious passbook back into my secret stash spot, a location I will never disclose in writing (just in case someone finds where I hide my journal), and then I called Myrna. I had no idea what I was going to say, and when my call went to messaging, I simply hung up. I mean, what was I going to say? "Help me, Myrna. My mom is out getting high again"?

About fifteen minutes later my phone rang, and it was Myrna.

"I noticed you called me," she said. "But you didn't leave a message."

"Sorry...I wasn't sure what to say."

"What's up?"

"I just needed someone to talk to."

"Uh-huh..." She sounded like she was doing something. Or maybe she was with someone.

"I didn't mean to bother you," I said quickly.

"How about doing lunch again?"

"Lunch?"

"Yes. Then we can talk."

"Okay..."

"Let me check my BlackBerry." She paused and I waited. "Do you work on Monday?"

And so it was set. We'd meet at the same restaurant. But I have no idea what I'll say to her. Maybe nothing. Maybe we can just chitchat.

August 19

I met Myrna for lunch today. My plan was to keep my mouth shut about Shannon, but Myrna pressed, and I finally just told her the whole thing. I explained how Shannon had completed nearly a full month of rehab and then, just like that, had returned to drugs.

"At least I'm fairly sure that's the case, although I haven't actually asked her. But all the signs are there. She goes missing. Comes home a couple of days later. Acts like she's got the flu or something and then gets better, and a day or two passes, and she takes off again. She was still around this morning, but I have no idea if she'll still be there when I get home from work."

"That's hard." Myrna shook her head. "And I know exactly how you feel."

"You do?"

Myrna told me about her son, Phil. "He's in his thirties now, and he's stayed clean. But back when he was using... well, he put my husband and me through the wringer. It's one of the reasons my marriage fell apart. We just couldn't take it."

"How did Phil get clean?"

"It was his third stint of rehab, a three-month inpatient treatment program in Colorado. It was designed for young men and included lots of hiking and outdoor things.

Something about all that fresh air and sunshine worked. Phil's been clean about seven years now."

"That's great. But I doubt my mom would want to do a program like that."

"So how do you manage to get by, Maya?" Her eyes looked truly concerned. "I mean, with Shannon out using and your dad on the road, who takes care of you?"

I had to laugh at that. "Takes care of me?"

"Well, I know you're not exactly a child, but you're not an adult either."

"The truth is, it feels more like I take care of Shannon." And suddenly tears burned in my eyes. But no way did I want to start crying here. Instead, I began to angrily pour out more of my story, going into detail about how irresponsible Shannon is, how she doesn't pay the bills regularly, how collectors call, how I'm responsible for myself. And finally I tell Myrna about my plan to be emancipated.

"Goodness, Maya, I had no idea things were so bad for you. Does your father know?"

Realization hit me then. What if Myrna informed my dad? What if he told Shannon? Oh, he wouldn't do it to hurt me, but it would mess things up.

"I haven't told him yet. And I don't want to tell him...not until I have things in place. He needs to focus on his tour."

"What kinds of things do you need to have in place?"

I told her what the social worker told me when I was thirteen. "So my plan is to save enough money to get my own place when I turn sixteen. And maybe I can get a car, and I'll keep on working and—"

"How is that even possible? Do you realize how much it would cost to support yourself? And how will you continue to work full-time once school starts up again?"

"I do homeschool."

"Who supervises your homeschooling?"

I shrugged. "Me."

"Do you honestly think a social worker will agree to this?"

I frowned now. "I hope so."

"Listen, Maya, you need a better plan."

"I do?"

"Absolutely. And I think I have one."

"What?" Did Myrna want to adopt me?

"Modeling."

I let out an exasperated sigh.

"Hear me out, sweetie. Models make excellent money. And they don't have to work the long hours you're putting in now."

"Really?"

"Would I lie to you?"

"Tell me more."

So Myrna explained how she could help me get signed at an agency owned by her friend and how I would likely have no problem getting work. "You could probably make enough money modeling to really support yourself, and then no one would question your plans to be on your own... if that's the way you finally decide to go."

"I just know I can't go on living with Shannon when she's like that. It's too hard. And it's scary too."

"But what about your dad?"

"He's too busy for me right now."

"You're probably right. It's not easy to revive a music career."

"And I'm willing to work. I've been working forty-hour weeks since June."

"Yes, but you won't be able to keep up with that and your schooling. Let me give my friend a call and see if you can go in and meet her. When's your next day off?"

"Tomorrow actually." Then I glanced at my watch. "But I need to get back to work now."

"Well, I'll call you after I talk to my friend and let you know how it goes."

"Thanks, Myrna." I stood and placed my napkin on the table. "Thanks for everything."

As I hurried back to work, I wondered if what she was suggesting was even possible. Oh sure, I'd gotten some nice attention at work. And occasionally people would ask me about my interest in modeling. But I always just brushed those comments off. Besides the fact that I don't think I'm very attractive and don't have the confidence for something like that, I hate the idea of parading myself around to be goggled at…or worse, criticized. Furthermore, I am not terribly fond of the fashion industry—okay, that's a huge understatement. I mean, seriously, why would I even consider something like that?

On the other hand, if I could earn enough money to get away from Shannon…well, that changes things. When I got home from work today, she was gone again. Big surprise there. So I'm telling myself that modeling, similar to working in retail, might simply be a temporary measure. A means to a better place. Just one more compromise on this rocky road of life.

So by the time Myrna calls, I am hoping that her friend with the agency will want to see me. And as it turns out, she does.

"The agency is called Montgomery's. As I told you, my friend Felicity is the owner. Felicity Montgomery. She used to be with the Ford agency. But she finally got the nerve and the money to start up her own. And she's already making a good name for herself in the industry. But she's very selective about her clients, and she doesn't even see people without a recommendation."

"I really do appreciate this," I tell her.

"Unfortunately, I won't be able to go with you. But it's in Beverly Hills and within walking distance. Well, for a young thing like you, that is. I myself would drive."

"I don't mind walking."

So she gives me the address. "Your appointment is for ten o'clock. And do not be late. If there's one thing Felicity will not tolerate, it's tardiness."

"I'll be there before ten."

"Good."

"Uh...what do I wear? I mean, is it kind of like an interview?"

"Just look nice and neat. Most important is that you're well groomed, Maya. Not that you're not usually. But clean hair and nails. Not too much makeup, not that you have that problem. If you look like you did at lunch today, you'll be just fine."

"Okay..."

"And just be yourself. No need to put on any pretenses with Felicity. She's sharp, and she can see right through people anyway."

So I thank her again and hang up. I feel nervous, and that bugs me. Really, modeling is stupid. Just a means to an end. And if Felicity Montgomery doesn't like me, it's no big deal. I still have my job at Ralph's. Even so, the idea of making more money—enough money to live on my own—well, that's slightly intoxicating. Freedom is calling.

Maya's Green Tip for the Day

Most girls my age enjoy the latest, greatest personal products. But how about trying something more natural—and cheap? Did you know that a little baking soda mixed with water makes great whitening toothpaste? And it's also a good mouthwash. Just half a teaspoon in a glass of water, and your breath will be fresher than ever. And if you have smelly shoes, you can pour a few tablespoons of baking soda into a pair of old socks, then put them in the shoes, and by morning they should smell a whole lot better.

Ten

August 20

I was very nervous as I waited to see Felicity Montgomery this morning. I got there five minutes before ten and then waited for nearly half an hour as Ms. I-Don't-Tolerate-Tardiness was running late. During that time I sat stiffly on a hard plastic chair, pretending to read a fashion rag but actually watching as young people, both guys and girls, came and went through the office. They were obviously models, and although they didn't give me the time of day, I couldn't help but study them.

And as I studied them, I came to the realization that (1) I did not fit in with these people, (2) I would never fit into their fashion scene, and (3) the sooner I got out of this place, the better for everyone. I was about to sneak out the door when the receptionist informed me that Ms. Montgomery would see me now.

Her office was starkly modern with pale, glossy wood floors and chairs that, like in the reception area, were molded plastic, shiny and black. Several chrome-framed shots of models adorned the white walls, and her desk was glass and chrome with very little on top. She seemed to be coordinated with her office in a sleek black dress and a long silver pendant as the only accent, well, besides a pair of black-rimmed glasses that gave her a stern look. Her hair was glossy silver and straight, cut short in the back and long in front, which in my opinion accentuated a rather long nose. Still, she was attractive in a severe fifty-something sort of way—the kind of looks that demand respect.

Anyway, I was glad that I'd worn black today since it seemed to be her favorite color. Quick introductions were made, and I could tell that she expected me to call her Ms. Montgomery. Then she told me to sit in the hard plastic chair across from her. I sat down, keeping my back straight but unsure what to do with my legs. I wanted to cross them but wasn't sure if that was proper.

"Maya Stark..." She said my name slowly. "Nick Stark's daughter, I understand."

I nodded without saying anything. Really, what was there to say?

She peered curiously at me now. "So tell me, Maya Stark. Why does Nick Stark's daughter wish to become a model? The truth, please."

I looked evenly back at her and remembered what Myrna had told me last night—this woman didn't want any attitude. And I didn't plan to give her any.

"The truth is, I never really wanted to be a model. I just need to make money, and Myrna suggested modeling."

Her narrow brows arched ever so slightly. "And why does Nick Stark's daughter need to earn her own money?"

"To live."

She picked up a silver pen now, holding it like a cigarette and rocking it between her fingers. "Have you any experience?"

So I told her about working at Ralph Lauren's and how I often wore the clothes there. "That's kind of like modeling, isn't it?"

She nodded, then wrote something down with her silver pen.

"Look," I said quickly, knowing that this wasn't only crazy but futile, "I'm obviously not the model type, and I don't want to waste your—"

"Hush."

So I shut my mouth and waited.

"I seriously doubt whether you know enough about fashion to determine who is and who is not 'the modeling type,' as you put it. But I have more than thirty years of experience in this industry. How about you let me be the judge of that? Now stand up."

"Huh?"

"Do not say 'huh.'"

"Pardon me?"

"Stand up."

So I stood.

"Now walk."

I took a breath, then walked across the floor, turned around when I was nearly to the wall, and walked back.

She gasped. "Good grief."

"What?"

"You walk like a farmer."

"Why, thank you," I said a bit smugly. "I do have a garden, and I wouldn't mind—"

"Hush! Now turn around. Do a slow three-sixty."

So I slowly turned.

"Hold your chin up."

I held my chin up.

"How tall are you?"

"I…uh…I'm not sure." I was flashing back to Vivian and the comments she'd made about my height. Still, I knew that height was an advantage in this part of the fashion world.

"And I suppose you don't know how much you weigh either?"

"Well, no…"

"Do you happen to know what size you wear?"

"In Ralph Lauren clothes I'm a four."

She wrote this down, then picked up her phone. "Marla, I need you to get the stats on a girl for me. Do you have time?"

She paused. "Yes, now! Of course, I mean now. Fine, I'll send her over." Then she slammed down the phone and swore. "Imbecile."

I was still standing there, wondering what I was supposed to do next. And she was still sitting there just staring at me.

"You put me in an awkward position, Maya."

"Why?"

"Most people who come in here actually wish to model. That doesn't seem to be the case with you."

I considered this. "It's not that I'm unwilling—"

She laughed now. Kind of a cackly laugh. "Honestly, I should send you packing."

"It's just that I had never dreamed of modeling...you know?"

"But you're willing..."

"Yes. And I would work hard. I've been working all summer, and I know how to work hard."

"Do you?" She looked skeptical.

"You're probably thinking that as Nick Stark's daughter, I've had a privileged life. Well, you're wrong about that. If you don't believe me, ask Myrna."

She seemed surprised by this.

"Look, I'm going to lay my cards on the table with you, Ms. Montgomery. My mother is an addict. My dad is on the road. I am working so I can be emancipated from my parents.

I want to live on my own and support myself. I'm practically doing that now."

She leaned forward, and her brow creased with what seemed genuine interest. "Is that so?"

"Yes. My plan is to be on my own by the time I turn sixteen. But to do that, I need money."

She nodded. "When do you turn sixteen?"

"December twelfth."

She made note of this too. "And what about schooling?"

I explained how I'd been doing homeschool. "I've been using a curriculum that's supposed to be pretty good."

"And are you smart?"

"Smart?"

"Yes, that's what I asked."

"I guess that depends on how you define smart. When I was in public school, I was identified as gifted. Not that it means much."

"Have you considered taking an equivalency test?"

"What's that?"

"Some call it a GED, a general equivalency diploma. You take a test that assesses your education. Some of our younger models do that in lieu of graduating from high school proper. A GED allows you to work as you like and to proceed on to college when you're ready to do so. So many of our models are young, and it's difficult to model and attend school regularly. Well, that's if you're a good model and in demand. Getting your GED is an easy way to keep everyone happy."

"Oh..."

"Just something to consider, that is if you're seriously considering modeling."

"I don't know if I could be seriously considered."

She laughed again, only that time it sounded a bit merrier. "I'm offering to represent you, Maya."

"You are?"

"Yes. But only if you give me your word that you will take this seriously."

"Of course."

"Because I doubt that you have a portfolio yet."

"A portfolio?"

"Sample photos, comps, that sort of thing."

"No..."

"My agency will help you put this together, but once you start being paid, we will deduct this expense from your checks. Do you understand?"

"But I will make money, right?"

"If you do good work...if people want you."

"In the meantime, can I keep my job at Ralph Lauren?"

"It will make scheduling you awkward."

"But I need to make money."

"Then I'm sure you'll want to work hard for us, because that is where your opportunity to make money lies, Maya."

"You think people would actually hire me?"

"I'm rather certain of it, but it's a risk you need to be willing to take yourself. And that means you should probably give your notice at Ralph Lauren. I expect that you could have jobs to do two weeks from now."

I nodded and swallowed hard. Was this a risk I was really willing to take?

"Go see Marla, and she'll get you set up."

I still had questions, but I could tell I'd been dismissed, so I stood and thanked her.

"That's all," she said crisply as she picked up her phone.

Of course, I didn't know who Marla was or where to find her, but the receptionist, a thin blonde named Katy, pointed me in the right direction. And before long I was being weighed and measured by a Nazilike woman. Marla Eisenberg. Without the slightest bit of warmth, she snapped orders and then frowned as she measured my chest, waist, and hips. Then she let out these big sighs as she wrote the numbers down, as if there was something terribly wrong with my dimensions. And suddenly I wondered if I could trust these people. Maybe I should rethink that bit about giving notice on my job.

"Stand up straight," she snapped at me as she measured my height, which turned out to be five foot ten and a half. I tried to cooperate, but the whole time I wondered why someone like Felicity Montgomery put up with someone like Marla. Besides being cranky, she didn't seem to have the slightest bit of fashion sense. In fact, I wasn't even sure what her job at the agency was. Mostly I just tried to get it over with and get out of there.

As I passed through the reception area heading straight for the door, Katy called out. "Wait, Maya. I have something for you."

"Oh?" I went back to her desk, and she handed me a shiny black folder.

"There are some forms to fill out, tax stuff and whatever. Also, that yellow card on top has information on your photo shoot appointment."

I opened the folder and looked at the yellow card. "Photo shoot?"

"You know, for your portfolio. Sounds like you're on the fast track."

"Oh." I nodded like this was not a surprise.

"Anyway, you better head over there. The only time Yuri could take you was at 11:45, and that's like five minutes from now."

"Five minutes?"

"No problem, his studio is just a couple of blocks down. Turn left on Crescent."

So feeling slightly out of breath, I arrived at the photo studio on time, and the next thing I knew, Yuri was shooting me.

Of course, I had no idea that I would need to change outfits for this shoot. Fortunately, Yuri's assistant, Danika, had a whole rack of items to choose from. She also helped me with makeup. It seemed she had done some modeling herself.

"We left Ukraine for better life," she explained as she fiddled with my hair. "Modeling paid our way. Then I have baby and retire." She patted her tummy. "And Yuri's photography took off."

I felt extremely uncomfortable and self-conscious when Yuri first started pointing the camera at me, but thanks to Danika's constant cheerful chatter, I began to relax until I was almost unaware that he was taking pictures.

"A swimsuit?" I said as Danika handed me a slinky, one-piece black suit.

"Your portfolio is not complete without swimsuit shot. But no worries, Maya. You have beautiful figure."

I reluctantly put on the swimsuit but then refused to leave the dressing room. Finally, after I explained to Danika that the high cut of the suit was making me uncomfortable, she allowed me to use an oversize silk scarf as a cover-up.

"But you must get bikini wax," she said quietly before I went out.

Okay, that was humiliating. But I guess the rest wasn't so bad. And I really liked Yuri and Danika. As it turned out, they sacrificed their lunch break just so they could shoot more photos of me.

"She is so beautiful," Danika assured her husband as they were finishing up. "When she is on cover of *Vogue*, we will say we shot her first."

"We'll send the photos to Montgomery's," Danika told me as I was leaving. "Probably early next week or sooner. Ms. Montgomery said to rush."

"I'm sorry you missed lunch."

"Missing a meal will not harm my waistline." Danika smiled at the girl in the waiting area, a pretty redhead with freckles and huge green eyes. "You're next, Campbell," she told her, then quickly introduced us. "Campbell is another one of our favorite girls. She's with Montgomery's too. Maybe you girls will work together soon."

After I left, I stopped at a nearby deli and asked the man behind the counter if Yuri and Danika ever ate there.

"Oh yeah, those guys are the best."

So I asked him to fix something they'd like. "And can you have it delivered?"

"No problem."

Then I paid him, put a tip in the jar, and left. I didn't care if they knew it was from me or not; it just felt good to repay their kindness. Kind of like karma. What comes around goes around. Or so they say...

Maya's Green Tip for the Day

Have you noticed how so many foods are "conveniently" packaged in these fancy-schmancy plastic containers? But did you know that these one-time-use containers not only make products cost more but also contribute a huge amount of waste to landfills? Why not look for foods that don't use so much packaging. And here's the other payoff—they will probably contain fewer preservatives and be healthier for you!

Eleven

September 20

It's been a month since I signed with the Montgomery Agency. And my savings account is just starting to show it. Ms. Montgomery set me up for some training, but only after I agreed to quit my job at Ralph Lauren. I wasn't so sure at first…it seemed like a risk to say good-bye to a paying job. But this last week I've had three different appointments as well as several callbacks for next week.

But here's the strangest part about all this. Shannon. Okay, I thought she might be a teeny-tiny bit excited about this new development in my life. Because for one thing, Shannon adores fashion and clothes. Besides that, she's picked on me for years for not caring about my appearance, and now I have to care, and she doesn't seem to even notice. And finally, Shannon loves fame and fortune. At least that's the impression I've always gotten from her. Well, unless she's in her binge mode and not conscious of anything besides getting her next hit. Otherwise, Shannon pays careful attention to who's who in Hollywood. She reads the magazines and gossip rags and always has her own spin on why someone is or isn't doing well. It's like she's the expert on everyone's life, well, except her own. So you'd think she might be slightly interested in her daughter's "modeling career." Not that I plan on being famous or rich or even on doing this for long. But just the same, I would've expected a little more enthusiasm from her. Maybe even a little support. Ha!

To make this thing even more confusing, she's been staying clean lately. And she's been attending her rehab meetings. Of course, being clean can make her pretty grumpy too. And maybe that's why she's acting so weird about this. Sometimes I almost think she's jealous. Like when I finally got her to go with me to the Montgomery Agency in order to sign the parental release form. Ms. Montgomery had been nagging me for a week to get this done.

"I can't imagine this will go anywhere for you." Shannon spoke loudly enough for anyone in the office to hear her. Not that anyone was listening. We were in the waiting room, and she'd been acting kind of snooty and arrogant, like she was so much better than everyone else there, like this agency was just a hole in the wall.

"Kind of small potatoes, isn't it?" she said when we walked in. Naturally, I pretended not to hear. I hadn't bothered to tell her that Felicity Montgomery had previously been with the

Ford agency or that she represented some pretty big West Coast names. I mean, what would be the point?

Despite Shannon's superior attitude, I hadn't missed how she had really fixed herself up for this appointment. Her hair was styled, and she was dressed impeccably in one of her favorite designer outfits. Okay, I thought she looked pretty slutty in it, especially considering her age, but I could tell by how she was walking that she was feeling good about herself. Maybe she thought they'd offer to represent her too. And maybe that would be a good thing...help keep her clean and sober. I mean, who knows?

"So you're Maya's mother," Ms. Montgomery said when we were seated in her office.

"Yes." Shannon made a dramatic little sigh. "My daughter informs me that she *wants* to be a model."

Ms. Montgomery cleared her throat, then looked directly at me. I knew she was remembering my confession that I did *not want* to be a model and that I simply wanted to make money—and be emancipated. I was holding my breath just then, but thankfully, Ms. Montgomery did not mention this. Instead, she got right to business.

"Because Maya doesn't drive," she began, "there is some natural concern about her making her appointments on time. Punctuality is crucial in this industry. As they say, time is money. So, Mrs. Stark, do you intend to act as Maya's chauffeur?"

Shannon laughed in an incredulous way. "Maya's chauffeur?"

"Maya will need reliable transportation and sometimes on short notice. We need to be assured that—"

"I know how to use public transportation," I said quickly. "And I have a bike, and if I had to, I could always call a taxi."

Ms. Montgomery adjusted her black-rimmed glasses and peered curiously at me.

"Maya is a resourceful girl," said Shannon smugly, "and very mature for her age."

"Yes…" Ms. Montgomery slowly nodded. "I can see that."

"I suppose most young girls dream of becoming models or actresses," Shannon continued lightly, almost as if she were the guest of a talk show and the camera was pointed at her now. "They have such a sense of entitlement anymore, assuming that celebrity comes easily." She laughed. And then she went on about her acting career, painting it much larger than it had ever been. Then finally saying, sadly, how her career had been cut short when she married.

"I was at my prime, and Nick wouldn't take no for an answer."

Ms. Montgomery's expression was a mixture of irritation and interest. And she just let my mom continue to ramble. I wanted to disappear.

"Nick didn't want me to continue my acting career. His

music was so demanding. And then, of course, Maya came along, and I was cast in a new role…as mother." Then, almost as if she really thought she was at an acting audition, Shannon actually tossed a maternal smile in my direction.

"Yes…" Ms. Montgomery quickly slid the paperwork across her desk. "Now, Mrs. Stark, if you could simply read this over, at your leisure of course, and sign the portions where the contract has been flagged, we'll be all—"

"I'll sign it now." Shannon reached for her bag, fumbling until she found a pen. Then without reading a single line, she signed the papers and slid them back. "Anything else?"

"Not really." Ms. Montgomery glanced at me. "Except that I'd like to meet with Maya briefly now."

"Without me?" Shannon blinked, then looked slightly offended.

"Of course you may stay if you like, Mrs. Stark. But I'm sure you'd be bored, and a busy woman like you must have a hundred other things to do. I hate to waste your time."

"Well, yes…I suppose so." Shannon stood, then looked curiously at me. Did she expect me to beg her to stay?

"Don't worry. I can walk home," I said.

So Shannon left, and despite everything, I found myself feeling slightly sorry for her again. She seemed so out of place in there. Such a total misfit. But to be fair, I think we're both misfits. Maybe that's just the way we were meant to be.

After Shannon was gone, Ms. Montgomery told me that my portfolio had come back. "It looks quite nice, Maya. You can pick it up from the front desk."

Then she explained about tear sheets, the photo samples I'm supposed to leave behind after appointments, and call-backs, meaning that someone liked my tear sheet and wants to see me again. She also told me how it was vital to always be accessible and how I should check in with the agency every morning by nine. She filled me in on some financial details, explaining how the agency would cover my expenses for training, which I was supposed to start the next day, as well as a few other things (like beauty supplies).

"We realize these are costly, but they are necessary," she told me. "And like your portfolio, the expenses will be deducted from your first checks."

Consequently, although it seemed like I should've made a lot of money, my first agency check, which I got today, was not very impressive. After the agency's percentage, the photo shoot, the portfolio, and various other expenses were deducted, I made even less than I would've earned at Ralph Lauren.

"That's not bad," Campbell Klopstein told me this after-noon. "Good grief, it took me three months to break even with the agency. My parents thought I was nuts not to quit."

"Really?" I studied her. She was so pretty and confident and, according to what I'd been hearing, in great demand in the L.A. fashion world. It was hard to imagine a model like her just scraping by.

"Fortunately, I was still living at home back then. But after a year or so, I knew I'd made the right choice."

We were on a callback for a new cosmetic line. I wasn't sure if we were in competition with each other or if they were considering using both of us. But I realized if it was a competition, Campbell would probably come out on top. Not only is her skin flawless, other than the freckles, but she has this most amazing nose. Small and narrow and, I'm guessing, very photogenic. And I had just gotten a zit on my chin. Still, I knew better than to concentrate on this flaw. A blemish could be covered or airbrushed. Welcome to the plastic world of fashion.

So as we sat there, I tried to remember some of the things I'd been learning. Ways to relax and give the camera your best. In some ways it felt like a mind game. And I'd been doing my "mirror work" (something I'd learned in one of my training sessions). The goal is to spend five minutes or less in front of the mirror while you practice smiling in a natural way. And while you do this, you concentrate on how your facial muscles feel so that when you're in front of the camera, you can do it again. You can also do it with body poses. Whether it's tilting a shoulder or placing a hand on the hip, there are ways that look natural and comfortable and ways that just make you look stupid.

At first I found this whole thing degrading and humiliating, like I'm a puppet that's being paid to perform. Or worse, a piece of meat that's being used to sell something I would never in a million years purchase myself. It all goes so against the grain with me. But it's the price I must pay for now.

As it turned out, Campbell and I had both been selected for the cosmetic company shoot. First they shot us together and then separately. It took most of the day. And afterward we went out and got coffee.

"How long have you been modeling?" I asked.

"I was about your age when I started. I'll be nineteen next month. Do the math."

"Do you plan to continue?"

"Sure." She grinned. "It's not a bad life, you know. The money's good, and the hours are doable. Why wouldn't I keep doing it?"

I shrugged. "I don't know…"

"You mean am I worried I'll get too old?"

"No, that's not what—"

"Because it's not like I'm delusional. I'm fully aware that most girls can't do this for long. And I've considered going to New York…"

"Why?"

"To broaden my career, of course. That's where it's really happening."

"Oh…"

"But I hate to leave my boyfriend."

I nodded. "Is it serious?"

She laughed. "It is with me, and I'm hoping it is with him too."

I tried to imagine how it would feel to be serious about a guy. I mean, I've had secret crushes but never anything I would call serious.

"We moved in together last summer, and I know it sounds crazy at my age, but I could imagine being married to Gray." She sighed happily. "I mean, we are so perfect for each other. He's this really organized and slightly geekish dude, and I'm totally the opposite—crazy and messy and spontaneous."

"And you actually get along?"

"Like peanut butter and jelly." She grinned. "And I'm the jelly."

"Oh..."

Then she started telling me more about some of the pitfalls of modeling, things to watch out for and people to trust or not to trust. I was almost tempted to take notes. Hopefully, I could remember all this.

"Am I overloading you?" she said finally, glancing at her watch.

"No. I really appreciate the inside information."

"Well, feel free to call me if you ever need to chat or want to know something about somebody. I may have only been doing this for three years, but I pretty much know the dirt on everyone by now."

Then we exchanged business cards, the ones provided by the agency, with their number as well as our cell phones. And we went our separate ways. She went home to Gray, and I went home to see if Shannon was still around. To my surprise, considering it's a Friday night, she was. But not surprisingly, she was holed up in her room.

In some ways Campbell is the closest thing to a friend I've had in a long time. Of course, I doubt she sees it that way. I mean, it's not like she invited me to call her up so we could just hang. Besides being a lot older than me, she's involved in a serious relationship. I'm sure that takes a lot of her spare time. Still, it would be nice to have a real friend.

October 14

Once again Shannon and I are like two ships in the night. I'm pretty sure she's using again, although I have no idea why. Well, other than the fact that she's an addict. But really, it seemed like life had smoothed out here for us. She actually paid some bills, and the house wasn't a total disaster. In fact, she almost seemed happy. And I almost felt hopeful.

But then she started to complain about being bored. Sometimes I wonder if she's bipolar. I don't know much about it, other than it causes mood swings. And even after I read about it on the Internet, I couldn't be sure. It seems like there are a lot of different kinds of bipolar. Plus, using drugs and alcohol can really complicate detection. I suspect she's a combination of a lot of things. I just wish she'd grow up and get over it. However, I doubt that's going to happen anytime soon.

The good news is that I'm making *good* money now. Okay, on some levels it feels like *bad* money. Or maybe just dirty money. Because, like Campbell warned me, there are some skanks in this industry. I'm sort of surprised at how many people assume that because I'm modeling, I'm also willing to sell my soul to the devil. Although to be fair, I'm not so sure there is a devil…or a God. Anyway, it's sad how models get a reputation for certain things like wanting to have sex with a photographer or stylist or the slimeball doing the lighting. I try to make myself perfectly clear around certain forms of lowlife. And Ms. Montgomery has made it known that she doesn't want her models compromised in any way.

Naturally, I never point out just how compromised I feel every time I pose in front of a camera. I figure that's my problem. In a way I am prostituting myself for money. Okay, I'm not having sex, but I'm selling my body and my face. And it really makes me sick. This whole industry makes me sick. And I hope that as soon as I'm free, I will find a more wholesome line of work.

Speaking of emancipation, I took my GED test and passed with flying colors. I actually studied for it and was surprised at

how easy it was. Still, it feels weird to be finished with high
school—without having gone one day. And it makes me sad.
And lonely.

Maya's Green Tip for the Day

Did you know that some shoe companies—the same
ones that charge you more than $150 for a pair of
shoes—might not be paying their workers a living
wage? A worker in India might be making less than $2 a
day to make those great-looking, big-name shoes. That's
why when you see a Fairtrade symbol on a product, you
can feel good about your purchase. You know that you're
not contributing to wage slavery in another country.

Twelve

November 28

It's Thanksgiving today. Not that anyone in this house pays attention to such traditional nonsense. And not that I care since I don't eat turkey and since I feel this holiday is simply the celebration of white people taking over a country that would've been better off without them. But that's just my take on it. Still, I can't help but wonder about the whole family thing. The image of happy American families gathering to—gag—eat meat and watch football games is slightly intriguing. Even to a vegan.

Anyway, I would probably be totally depressed by the fact that I pretty much have no family and Shannon is AWOL again...except for one thing. I got paid yesterday, and it was the biggest check yet. My savings account has more than ten thousand dollars in it now! I know that doesn't sound like much to some people, but I feel like a millionaire.

The other thing that makes me extremely happy is knowing my birthday is only two weeks away. Emancipation day! Okay, not exactly. But it's the day I intend to file. And I've already done the research and have a plan that will pressure both my parents into agreeing. Sure, some might call it black-mail. Particularly Shannon. But I simply call it a full disclosure of the facts unless they both sign on the dotted line.

And if all goes well, I will soon be on my own! I've already started to look for another place to live. At this point I think I'll try to rent a room somewhere nearby. Although I did find a studio for less than eight hundred dollars a month. If I could find someone to live with me, it might work. Not that anyone is stepping up to offer. Still, I'm keeping my eyes open. And if I take a roommate, I will make sure that she doesn't do drugs or alcohol. And that she has a respectable job. Not that I consider mine terribly respectable, but that could change in the new year.

On the other hand, if I moved out of Beverly Hills, I might save money. But then there's the transportation thing. To get to jobs, if I keep modeling, I would probably need a car. And although I've been studying for my license, there are some obstacles. Like drivers' training, which I haven't had. Also, I don't even have a learner's permit yet. Anyway, I'm not sure I'll ever be able to afford a car. Even a cheap car, with gas and insurance, would tap my budget. Sometimes, like today, I wonder why a fifteen-year-old girl has to figure these things out.

Really, shouldn't I be out in the backyard tossing a foot-ball around with my dad and siblings? Waiting for Mom to finish roasting the turkey? Whipping that cream to top the pumpkin pie? Like I'd even want to eat such things. On the other hand, and this is the honest truth, I would probably exchange my vegan lifestyle to be part of a traditional American family. Not that I think they exist. It's probably just an old fairy tale. Or something that people pretend to live up to.

December 2

To the tune of two hundred dollars, I met with a lawyer today. Her name is Jeannette Williams, and she advised me on my emancipation. According to her, I have a pretty good case.

"Here are the basic criteria," she told me. "You must be at least fourteen."

"Check."

"You must have a good reason not to live with your parents."

"Check."

"You must be in school until graduation."

So I explained about my GED certificate.

"That will work." She nodded and returned to her list. "And you must have a legal way to make your own money."

"Check."

"You must know how to handle your own money and budget."

"Check." This was actually not new to me. I'd read this much online. I was beginning to wonder if paying for legal advice was a waste. But Ms. Montgomery had recommended Jeannette to me, and I was trying to do this thing right.

"Emancipation would improve your life," she said.

I considered this. It could be a matter of perspective. "Well, it's fairly miserable living with my mom. I mean, there are times when it seems okay, but her addiction is pretty upsetting, not to mention unpredictable. And then she doesn't pay the bills on time. And I feel like I'm on my own anyway, except that I'm living with a loose cannon."

"I think you have a convincing case in that regard, Maya." She smiled. "And then, of course, your parents must be okay with the emancipation. If they don't sign off, you could end up with a long, drawn-out case. And I don't think you can afford that...not and have the funds you need to convince the court you can live independently from them. Does that make sense?"

"Yes."

So then she told me I didn't have to hire an attorney to do this, although I sensed she wasn't convinced I could really do it without a lawyer. "You can present your case yourself and ask a judge to declare you emancipated."

"And that's it?" I asked hopefully.

"Not quite. You must also give your parents notice that you are seeking emancipation. In writing."

"I can do that."

She gave me the name of a government Web site with the forms and petitions I would need to fill out, writing down the numbers of the forms I should download as well as the court fees and costs.

"Although you might do a waiver." Then she told me which form to use for that. "And you need to build your case."

Build my case? Okay, I was already feeling fairly confused, and I began to wonder if she wasn't purposely throwing too much at me, hoping I'd retain her for legal advice after all. Still, I continued to take notes, and she started rattling off another list. Things I would need to present to the judge, including a letter stating why I want emancipation, a letter from me stating that I know what emancipation is and that I asked about it of my own free will.

"My assistant will prepare a list and send it to you."

"Is that everything?" I asked, resisting the urge to wipe my brow and say, "Whew."

"You also need a letter from your employer stating where you work, what you make, how long you've worked there. And a pay stub. And since you're not renting yet, you should take something that proves you have a suitable place lined up. Also your bank statement."

"Okay..." I paused from my note taking to look up, and I'm sure I looked fairly overwhelmed just then.

"It's really not all that complicated," she finally said, "and you seem like a very smart girl. I'm sure you'll figure it out. But feel free to call my assistant if you have any more questions. And that Web site should be very helpful too."

"Thanks."

"And really, Maya, I'm sure you can handle it just fine." She shook my hand. "Normally, I wouldn't encourage a teen to take this action, but in your case I think it's appropriate. Just keep in mind that being emancipated does not give you all the same rights as an adult."

"Meaning?"

"Meaning you still have to abide by the law as it applies to minors. No drinking, you can't vote—things like that."

I smiled. "No problem."

"Good luck."

So I went home, and after carefully going over my notes again and checking out the Web sites until I had a fair grasp on all these details, I spent the rest of the day attempting to get my ducks in a row. And like Jeannette assured me, it's not really that complicated. Just a little overwhelming at first. And then time consuming. Perhaps the hardest thing was to write the letter to my parents. After several drafts that I scrapped, I finally decided to keep it unemotional and businesslike. It might be best not to rock their boats too hard. Well, unless they decide to rock back. Then I will let them have it!

December 6

This is the darkest day of my life. And that is not an exaggeration. No one died. Well, except for me. In many ways I feel that I am dead now. And I'm even considering how this might be accomplished in actuality. If Shannon's car were here, which it's not, I would go into the garage, close all the doors, open all the windows of the car, turn on the ignition, and just go to sleep. In fact, I might even sneak into a neighbor's garage. Who knows?

The day started out normal enough. I went to a photo shoot and subjected myself to the usual humiliation of being primped and fussed over, even getting my boobs taped into place, and then sweltering under the lights, I attempted to look cool and calm. Aloof was what the director was going for. I think I pleased him. What I won't do for the almighty dollar.

Then I went by the agency to pick up my check, my personal justification that compromising myself for money is marginally acceptable. After that, I went straight to the bank, just like I always do on Fridays. I waited in line, signed my check, pulled out my passbook, and made my deposit. But then the teller handed me my deposit slip, and just like always, I looked at the total. And then I blinked and looked again.

"Something is wrong," I told the teller, holding out the slip as if that should explain everything.

"What's that?"

"The amount." I pointed to the number on the bottom. "That's way off."

"Let me see." She took back my passbook and punched the numbers into her computer. "No, that's right, Maya. With what you just put in today, you now have a total of $985.65. Not bad."

"But I just put in $900!"

"Yes. That, along with the existing $85.65, makes it—"

"I had more than $10,000 in that account!" I was shouting, and I'm pretty sure everyone was staring at me.

She glanced over her shoulder. "Perhaps you'd like to speak to the manager. There are other customers waiting."

I nodded firmly. "I definitely want to speak to the manager."

I had to wait for what felt like an hour but was probably just minutes. The whole time I was fuming to think that the bank had somehow made a stupid mistake and had somehow misplaced all my money. But I had all my deposit receipts in the back of my passbook. And all my deposits were meticulously recorded. No big deal. I had what I needed to make them understand the situation.

"Can I help you?" asked a middle-aged woman in a navy blue suit.

I held up my passbook and quickly explained my dilemma. She asked me to come over to her desk, where she began to punch in numbers on her computer. She looked at the screen and nodded as if it all made perfect sense.

"Yes, Maya, you did have quite a bit more money in this account. But it seems that a rather large withdrawal was made only yesterday...a total of—"

"I wasn't even in the bank yesterday. It's a mistake. My money should all still be here."

"You are aware that your parents are cosigners on this particular account, aren't you?"

I considered this. "Well, my dad set it up for me when I was little. I guess that means he's a cosigner. But he wouldn't take my money."

"And your mother is a cosigner as well."

"My mom?" A chill followed by a wave of sickness washed over me, like I might throw up all over her desk.

"Apparently your mother made a withdrawal."

"And you let her?" My voice was so loud that the bank got quiet once again.

"It's a shared account, Maya."

"Not shared by me!" Tears of fury burned in my eyes. "Why did you let her take my money?"

The woman seemed very uncomfortable now. She lowered her voice. "It's not that we let her take your money. As a cosigner she had every right to withdraw the funds. Usually it's the parents who make most of the deposits in these accounts anyway, and we certainly can't stop them from—"

"I made every single deposit in that account!"

She stood and took me firmly by the arm as if she planned to lead me out. I even noticed her nod toward a security guard, who quickly joined us by the door.

"Need some help here?" he asked.

"I'm sure that you and your mother can sort this out at home," said the manager in a stern tone. "Perhaps your mother has simply transferred the funds into another account, perhaps a tax-deferred account or a college fund that could draw more interest. You really shouldn't be so—"

"No! You don't understand!" I raced out of the bank and ran all the way home. But when I got here, Shannon, of course, was gone. She'd been gone last night, and she was still gone. It didn't take a genius to figure out what she was up to.

So I went to her so-called office, which she rarely uses except as a place to dump the things she refuses to deal with. And I began to dig through the piles of junk mail and bills heaped on top of her desk. Some of the items were months old. There were a couple of bank statements for her, and not surprisingly, her account was overdrawn. Then I noticed a similar envelope in the garbage. My bank statement, which according to the postmark, had been sent out earlier this week. Shannon must've seen that I had mail from the bank, opened the envelope, discovered my money, and decided it was okay to steal it from me.

Then I noticed something else on her desk. A copy of my emancipation letter! I had planned to give it to her right after I filed with the court—next Monday. Shannon had obviously been snooping in my room. And she obviously knew about my plan! She probably went through the materials I'd put together to present to the judge.

And that's when I knew it was ruined. In one quick trip to the bank, Shannon had spoiled my perfect plan. I wanted to kill her. Seriously, if she had been in the room with me, if I'd had a gun, I would've shot her. I really think I would've. Not that I'm proud to admit this, but it's the truth.

Feeling desperate and hopeless and even dangerous, I called my dad and insisted on speaking to him. "It's an emergency!" I screamed at the person who was fielding his calls. "This is his daughter, and I have to talk to him! *Now!*"

When he finally came to the phone, I was sobbing like a baby, so hysterical that I could hardly speak. "Calm down," he kept telling me. "Take a deep breath, and tell me what's going on. Are you okay?"

I finally calmed down enough to speak. Between sobs, I told him everything. I told him the truth about Shannon's messed-up rehab and her return to using. I told him about the savings account and how Shannon had robbed me. I told him that I had planned to be emancipated and that she had found out and sabotaged me. And finally I told him that I was probably going to kill myself before the day was over. And then I hung up.

And even now...I'm not so sure that I won't kill myself. I can't think of one good reason to go on living. Not one. Life is not only unfair; it's too hard. And it just goes from bad to worse to impossible. I want to give up.

Maya's Green Tip for the Day

Who cares about the planet?

What's the point of even trying?

Why not just let the earth suffer? Go ahead and waste energy, pollute the air, pile up the landfills, poison the water...

What difference does it make?

Thirteen

December 9

Well, as it turns out, I am still alive. But only because my dad flew out here to the rescue. Because he had a concert on Saturday night, he couldn't come sooner. He offered to have someone else come to help me, but I told him I could manage. However, that was a lie. Anyway, I suppose it was good that he got here when he did. Otherwise I'd probably be locked up for murder right now.

Shannon got home Sunday afternoon (that was yesterday, two days after my darkest day). By then I had found her gun, which wasn't very well hidden, in the bottom drawer of her nightstand. At first I considered using it on myself, but then I decided that I'd wait for her to come home, and we could check out together. Yes, I know I was insane...and maybe I just wanted to scare her. Fortunately for both of us, the gun was hidden away in my room when she showed up in the middle of the day, catching me totally off guard.

"Hey, baby, what's up?"

I jumped up from the sofa where I'd been lying for hours, just staring at the ceiling. "Where's my money?" I demanded.

"What?" She gave me a fakey innocent look.

"My money!" I shrieked. "You stole it, and you know it."

"Oh, don't you mean *our* money, Maya?"

"Our money?" My face was so close to hers I could smell her bad breath. I was staring straight into her eyes, and if looks could kill, she would've been toast. *"That was not our money, Shannon! That was my money!"*

"Well, it was obviously money that Nick sent...so I would consider it as *ours.*" She put on her little pouty face now. "And I can't believe you've been holding out on me like that, Maya."

"That was not money from Nick! That was money I earned myself! Every single cent you stole from me was money I had worked for. And you deserve to go to jail for taking it. You are not only the world's worst mother, Shannon. You are a lying, cheating, crackhead thief!" Then I began to swear at her. And normally I don't use that kind of language, because I sound so much like her when I do, but I couldn't stop myself. I was in a rage—a total out-of-control rage.

Of course, my accusations and language only added heat to the fight. And before I knew it, we were both screaming and cussing, and she slapped me, and I slapped her back— hard! I was so enraged that I wanted to tear her hair out and scratch her face and all sorts of horrid things, and we were just about to really go at it, but someone was pounding on the front door.

"What's going on in there?" demanded a male voice. And

suddenly not only my dad but also a couple of his guy friends burst into the house and rushed into the living room, and after a brief scuffle, they managed to separate us before I had a chance to murder my mother.

And that's when I just totally lost it. With tears streaming down my face, I ran to Dad and fell into his arms. "I can't do this anymore," I sobbed. "I can't live like this anymore." I'm sure I said a lot of other hysterical things too, but I don't really remember. What I do remember is that Thomas, my dad's manager, took me to my room and somehow got me to calm down while Dad talked to Shannon.

"You're coming with us, Maya," Thomas told me in a kind voice. "Let's get whatever you need and get you out of here."

I could hear my mom and dad in the other room. Dad had picked up right where I'd left off, yelling and screaming and making all kinds of accusations. And I wouldn't have been surprised if it had evolved into a physical fight as well, although my dad has always been opposed to violence. Anyway, I'm sure we could've gotten a TV contract for our own reality show just then. Another one of those celebrity closeups about the dysfunctional family and how they get along.

"What is this?" Thomas had picked up my denim jacket to discover it was hiding Shannon's gun.

I just shrugged, and he shook his head as he unloaded the gun, then stuck it in his jacket pocket. "This has gone way too far," he muttered, "way too far..."

Finally I had a couple of bags packed, just stuffed with whatever was handy. Then I went out to the living room, where Dad and Shannon were still screaming at each other. And somehow Thomas and the other guy managed to drag my dad away from her and out of the house, and we all climbed into a black SUV and drove away.

And so it is that I'm on the road with my dad. Right now we're staying at a big hotel in Memphis. I don't know where we'll be after that. Mostly I've just been sleeping. I think I might sleep for a year or so. Or at least until I turn sixteen and figure out where to go from here.

January 3

It's been a surreal few weeks. Being on the road with my dad and his crew started out to be interesting. I mean, his tour bus (an enormous, luxurious motor home) is pretty cool, and I'm seeing some new places and meeting some new people, but it has gotten old surprisingly fast. We spend a few days in a city, then just when I get my equilibrium, we head off to another place. Sometimes we sleep on the road, and although my bunk is pretty comfy, I have a hard time actually sleeping. I feel a bump in the road or whatever, and I am wide awake. And then I start to feel seriously claustrophobic in my little bunk-bed closet—like I'm about to scream or something if I have to stay there another minute. But I don't want to get up and wander around because I'll disturb someone else. Very frustrating.

It's a little better when we stay in hotels, but that's usually only for a night or two. For one thing it's expensive, my dad has pointed out, but besides that, there's a schedule to keep. And keeping that schedule takes its toll on everyone. Mostly my dad. Although he's tried to be patient with me—and I know I'm an intrusion—he can easily get really grumpy. To be fair, he's not grumpy like Shannon, but he can say things without thinking. And I suppose I'm feeling more sensitive these days. Sometimes I wonder if I might need serious counseling or even a shrink.

And it doesn't help matters that I can barely remember where we are from one day to the next. Even though Dad gave me a map, I still wake up disoriented. And the worst part is that I miss being outside, puttering in the yard, sitting in the sunshine. Ordinary stuff like that. Oddly enough, I sort of miss Shannon too. That's what makes me think I need some psychological help. I must be crazy. But I've heard about Stockholm syndrome. And in some ways, living with Shannon was a little like that. Not that she held me captive, not physically anyway, but I did feel like I was trapped. And I still dream of emancipation.

Speaking of emancipation, I called the Montgomery Agency to explain that I wouldn't be working for them anymore.

"Why on earth not?" demanded Ms. Montgomery.

So I told her the truth, complete with details of how I wanted to murder my mother, and if my dad hadn't shown up, I might've.

"Oh, my..." I think she gasped.

"So you see, I'm with my dad now. He's touring, and I'm going along for the ride."

"It's unfortunate timing," she told me. "Your career was just beginning to heat up. We'll have to cancel your bookings."

"I'm sure someone else will be happy to have them." That was an understatement. After only a few months, I was well aware of the competition between models. Just joining the team had made me numerous enemies. In fact, Campbell was probably the only one who treated me half decent. And that's probably because she was still in demand.

"We'll miss you," said Ms. Montgomery.

And although my jaded side (yes, I realize I'm jaded, go figure) assumed she meant that she'd miss the money, I wondered if she really meant me...

And of course that reminded me of something, or rather someone. And to be fair it's someone I think of almost daily. And yet I've never written about her in this journal. But time's the only thing I have on my hands at the moment. Time and memories.

When my dad left, he didn't leave me completely. He invited Grandma Carolina to step in. Shannon protested at first. But only until she realized that Grandma Carolina could replace not only Nanny Jane but Francesca and Rosa as well. We'd been limping along for a couple of years by then, and our household was, shall I say, a shambles!

The weird thing was that I didn't even know I had a Grandma Carolina—or any kind of grandma, for that matter. But when my dad left, he made one condition: Shannon had to let his mother move in with us. This resulted in a horrible fight with Shannon making so many horrible accusations that I actually believed this Grandma Carolina was the devil incarnate. Okay, I was only seven; I'm sure that's not exactly what I thought. But the way my mom talked, I assumed she was like the bogeyman.

Consequently, it took me a while to warm up to this woman even though she reminded me a lot of my beloved Nanny Jane. But even at seven, I was becoming jaded. I didn't completely trust this woman—and Shannon treated her like a servant. Or perhaps like a slave. Grandma Carolina never complained. Not really. I mean, she would say things—make observations—but they weren't complaints. And strangely enough, she mostly seemed to have compassion for Shannon. In fact, I think that's what first won me.

One time Shannon was having a hissy fit about something. I think she wanted fresh coffee, and because she hadn't gotten up until noon, I suspect the coffee was a bit stale. Well, instead of making a fresh pot like a normal person, she threw a fit. And I watched in the shadows. But Grandma Carolina, instead of engaging with her, simply made a fresh pot. But as she made it, she sang a song. Some old hymn as I recall, and although I can't remember the words, I remember thinking that Grandma Carolina had been the winner of that round. But I didn't even know why. To be honest, I still don't know why. I just know that she came out on top. And in that moment, she had my full attention. Not that I wanted her to know it exactly.

After that I began to trail her around the house, and she would talk to me, almost the way a person might talk to a wild animal. Sort of softly and gently, nonintimidating, as if she knew I'd been through something. And eventually I started to respond. And before long we were the best of friends. In some ways—most ways—she was the closest thing to a mother I've ever had. No, she was my mother.

Grandma Carolina taught me to appreciate nature and how to garden. She knew the names of birds and trees and flowers. She knew how to make compost tea (fertilizer for plants), and she knew how to make biscuits that would melt in your mouth. And maybe best of all, she knew how to make Shannon happy. Or as close to happy as Shannon has ever been. But did Shannon ever thank her? Or show an ounce of appreciation? Yeah, right.

Instead, Shannon actually picked on Grandma Carolina when she was in a particularly bad mood. Sometimes Shannon even called her names—and I mean racial names—the kind of names that people would get into serious trouble for saying if anyone overheard them. Of course, I was the only one to overhear them. And I couldn't help but wonder if those names were not just for my grandma...but for me and my father as well.

Anyway, thanks to Grandma Carolina, who I later learned was born in South Carolina, my life from the age of seven to twelve was relatively cool. I mean, I still had Shannon to put up with, but having Grandma Carolina around was like having an anchor. Or something like that.

And during those years, we went to church. Not Shannon, of course. No, she always had an excuse. And no matter how Grandma Carolina hinted and hoped, it just didn't happen. For one thing Shannon never got up early enough. But besides that, I think she just didn't want to go. Maybe she didn't want to be seen with us. Maybe she wasn't comfortable with us.

And in fairness, Shannon would've stood out in that particular church—a fair, blue-eyed blonde amid a sea of African American faces. To be honest and despite my darker skin, I had moments when I felt out of place as well. I mean, most of my school friends at that time were white. And I suppose I thought of myself as being like them. They accepted me as one of them, and I went along for the ride. Well, mostly. It got a little dicey in middle school.

But the truth is, I never felt more at home and comfortable than I did standing with my grandma in her church. With her holding my hand as we sang some pretty lively songs. And then being around her friends, even if they were all a lot older than me. They were kind to me. They liked me. It was like family.

And when I was eleven, I went forward. I had considered going forward a number of times before. But I was a little bit stubborn. Finally I thought I "saw the light." And when Reverend Samuel gave the altar call, I stepped out into the aisle and went forward.

Well, Grandma Carolina couldn't have been more pleased if she had won the lottery. And she was known to buy tickets occasionally. Afterward, everyone patted me on the back and welcomed me into the "family of God." Reverend Samuel gave me a Bible, and it was great. But short lived.

Exactly one month later, in early December and shortly before my twelfth birthday, Grandma Carolina had a heart attack. I was at school when it happened, and I didn't even find out about it until I got home. And even then, Shannon didn't say much. Just that Grandma Carolina had been cleaning the oven...and died.

My dad came home for the funeral, and when he saw how distraught I was over her death, he explained that my grandmother had some pretty serious health problems—high blood pressure and cholesterol—and that she had known her time wasn't far off. That was why he had encouraged her to come live with us—so she could take it easy. Of course, I thought that was pretty ludicrous since Shannon had treated Grandma Carolina like a servant and maybe even hastened her death, but I never said as much. Not to anyone. I just silently grieved the loss of the best friend I'd ever had.

Life got worse after that. And although I'd given my heart to the Lord, I think I took it back. My reasoning was that if the Lord cared so little about me as to take the one person I really needed, well, why should I give a hill of beans for Him? So I don't.

Does this make me feel bad when I think of Grandma Carolina? Yeah, *duh*. For that reason I try to put both her and God out of my thoughts. But it's just not easy—I mean with her. As far as God goes...well, I don't think I care. If He really does exist, which I doubt, He's doing a pretty crummy job of taking care of His creation.

Maya's Green Tip for the Day

I know that my grandmother's death contributed to the fact that I am a vegan. And while I don't try to force my vegetarian values on everyone, there are some facts about meat consumption that should concern us all when it comes to our planet. (1) Grazing land uses about 26 percent of ice-free land on our planet. (2) Feed crops (for animals) use about 33 percent of all arable land on the planet. (3) Seventy percent of previously forested land in the Amazon is now being used as pasture for livestock. What this means is that if farmland was used for growing grains and vegetables for human food, not for feeding animals, there would be a lot more food for the planet to share. This is another reason I don't eat meat.

Fourteen

January 26

I hate to admit it, but I've developed what I'm afraid is a major crush on one of the roadies. His name is Jason, and he's twenty-seven. I know that's a lot older than me, but I'm pretty mature for my age. I seriously wonder if it could work. Also, I am keeping my age secret. He knows I'm still a teenager, but I'm hoping he thinks I'm more like eighteen. Now some people might not think Jason is the best-looking guy around, but I would have to differ with them. Besides being tall and fairly well built, he's got those classic features that could be found on a Michelangelo sculpture. Add to this some great dark, wavy hair that he wears tied back in a pony and a distinguished goatee, and the man is just about perfect! Not that I'm into looks. Really, it's his soul that attracts me. He's an artist and a musician. And he even likes to cook.

All we've done so far is talk. He's a great listener and has had some life experiences that seem to parallel my own. We are simpatico. He even said as much. Well, not in a romantic way. The problem is that although he's nice to me, he still treats me like a kid sister. Sometimes he teases (in a good-hearted way), and he's also very protective. And he's warned me that some guys on the crew are not to be trusted. Not that I'm worried. Mostly they just ignore me or look at me like I'm this huge nuisance, which is not the case.

"How long are you going to tour with us?" Jason asked this morning. We were having coffee in the hotel lobby, waiting for everyone else to check out so we could hit the road. I was hoping they'd take forever like usual. That way I'd get more time to talk with Jason. Unfortunately that wasn't the case.

"Get moving, Maya," commanded my dad when he showed up looking haggard and sleepy and like he'd forgotten to shave. "We're burning daylight here."

I wanted to point out that I'd been waiting for him, but he's been extra grumpy since New Year's. I know the reason is that he's working too hard—too many concerts—and I'm worried this tour is going to kill him. I even said as much to Thomas, who acted slightly concerned, then told me it wasn't really my problem. Okay, if it's not my problem, whose problem is it?

Speaking of problem parents, Shannon has been calling me on my cell phone for weeks now. At first I simply ignored her calls, then finally I felt guilty. I mean, even if I hate her, she is my mom. So about a week ago I answered. To my surprise the first thing she said was, "I'm sorry."

"Are you really?" I asked in what I know was a cold and suspicious tone.

"I am so sorry, baby. I know how badly I hurt you. And all I can say is that it was the drugs. It wasn't me."

Okay, I didn't know how to respond to that. I mean, who was the one who chose to use the drugs? Who was the one who chose to steal my money? Finally I said as much.

"You're right, Maya. You're absolutely right. And all those things you said to me that day...well, even though they hurt a lot, I know they were the truth. I'm a horrible person. A horrible mother. I've been nothing but a great big hopeless mess, and I can't blame you for hating me."

"Yeah..."

"Even so, I hope you can find it in your heart to forgive me...someday."

"I don't know..."

That was pretty much our first conversation, and I was extremely relieved to end it. But the next time she called, I was a tiny bit nicer. But that was only because I was in a good mood, thanks to Jason. We'd just had a great heart-to-heart talk about families and dysfunction. He came from a home where his dad got drunk and beat the kids on a regular basis. And yet Jason seems to have forgiven his dad and moved on. He even said that he uses the pain in his music. He's a songwriter as well as a pretty mean bass player, although he only does the grunt work on Dad's show.

As much as I respect Jason, I'm not sure I get the part about forgiving someone who's wounded you so deeply. And

I am absolutely certain that I can never put to use the crud that Shannon has dumped into my life. Mostly I just want to stay far, far away from her.

But thanks to Jason's influence, I answered the phone that day with a slightly cheerful voice, which I'm sure must've taken Shannon by surprise.

"Oh, baby," she said with a sob in her voice, "I miss you so, so much."

"You miss me?" Okay, the skepticism was back then. I seriously doubted that Shannon missed me. For the past few years she's been pretty much unaware of me. But maybe she missed my help in keeping things picked up. I could only imagine how the house looked by now.

"I miss you more than you can imagine, baby. My life is so empty without you."

I wanted to tell her that she sounded like she was singing the lyrics from one of Dad's songs, but I controlled myself. Instead I asked, "Are you staying clean?"

"I've been clean for thirty-two days now. And I've been going to the rehab meetings really regularly. I've even been spending time with Myrna."

"Myrna?" Now this surprised me.

"In fact, she told me to send you her love."

"Really?"

"Did you know her son was an addict?"

"Actually, I did." Okay, was it possible that our big blowout had done something in her—something that nothing else could do? Or was I just wishing? Anyway, we talked some more, and although I was cautious, I wondered if she might really be changing.

February 6

I had an interesting conversation with Dad about Shannon at dinner tonight. It was just the two of us for a change, and he was in a fairly good mood. We'd checked into a hotel in Grand Rapids earlier in the day, and he'd had a long nap and a soak in the Jacuzzi. I think he was feeling slightly rested, although he was also gearing up for tomorrow night's concert.

"I talked to Shannon again today," I told him.

"Has she fallen off the wagon yet?"

"No. In fact, she said she was celebrating Day Forty of sobriety today."

Dad toasted with his water glass. "Good for Shannon."

"Do you think she'll stick with it this time?"

He frowned, and I could tell he was even more skeptical than me.

"Why do you think she uses?" I asked.

"Wow, if I could answer that question, I might be able to write a self-help book and be on the *Dr. Phil* show."

"Seriously, Dad. You've known Shannon longer than I have. Why do you think she uses?"

"Because she's an addict."

"I know. But why is she an addict?"

"It might be a chemical imbalance."

"I've wondered about that too," I admitted.

"Or it might be her way of avoiding things." His expression was thoughtful now, as if he was seriously considering this.

"What things?"

"Shannon had a pretty sad childhood, Maya. Has she ever told you anything?"

I shook my head. "Not much."

"Her dad was a real creep."

"I know that she left home early to get away from him," I said.

"Well, after her mom died and her sister was gone, Shannon didn't have anyone to protect her from her dad."

"So he beat her?"

"And worse..." Dad looked uncomfortable now, like he didn't really want to talk about this. But I needed to know.

"Do you mean he sexually abused her?" I asked quietly.

"That's what Shannon told me once. She never wanted to talk about it though, and even when I encouraged her to get counseling, she'd get mad. Sometimes she'd even deny that it had happened. She'd accuse me of making the whole thing up." He looked sad.

"But you didn't..."

"No." The bill came then, and he signed it. "And I should warn you that Shannon could be mad at me for telling you that, Maya. But I think maybe you needed to know."

"Thanks, Dad. I probably won't ever mention it to her."

"You could get your head bit off if you did."

And I'm pretty sure he's right about that. At least about the old Shannon. To be honest, I am wondering if she might really be changing. Also, as I think about what my dad told me, I feel a little sorry for her. I don't know if I feel sorry enough to forgive her for everything, but I feel a bit more understanding than before.

February 15

I am perfectly miserable today. Dad fired Jason yesterday, and it was my fault. We were in Branson so Dad could perform a Valentine's Day concert last night. Jason had made a joke about how this was "the land of old people," and I thought he was kidding. But I looked around and realized he was right, which is odd since I don't think of my dad as terribly old. I mean, he's not ready for a walker or an oxygen bottle yet. But he must be in his sixties, which seems rather ancient if you think about it.

Anyway, it was a typical day. As usual, I'd been just hanging by myself while they got things set up, checking out the hotel amenities, which were also typical. And being that it was Valentine's Day, I noticed that the hotel gift shop had all kinds of romantic cards and goodies to give to your Valentine. So on impulse I decided to get a little something for Jason. Okay, I know it was probably stupid. But I was bored and surrounded by old folks who seemed to be having more fun than me. I guess I just couldn't help myself.

So I got Jason this cool card and a big milk chocolate heart wrapped in red foil. Then I went and found him working on the setup for the concert, and I presented my Valentine to him. Oh, in the meantime I'd also fixed myself up a little, so I looked pretty nice and probably older too.

Jason had been bugging me about my age lately, trying to figure out how old I really am, which made me think that he could be interested. But I just acted aloof and mysterious. I'd already told him that I was old enough to drive but not old enough to vote. I also told him that I had my GED, which makes me sound older.

Anyway, I was pretty sure we were alone backstage when I gave him the card and chocolate, and he seemed totally blown away by it.

"Wow, Maya, this is for me?"

"Sure," I told him, suddenly embarrassed to realize how much I'd shocked him, which meant he hadn't even considered me in a romantic way.

"Wow, that's really sweet of you." Then he opened and read the card, and I could tell he was slightly uncomfortable.

Maybe because I'd written "Love, Maya" at the bottom, along with an *X* and *O*. And suddenly I was pretty uncomfortable too, and for one long awkward moment, neither of us said anything.

"I guess it was kind of silly...," I admitted. "But it was Valentine's Day, you know, and—"

"I think it was really sweet," he said sincerely. "I will treasure it always."

Okay, that probably bolstered my confidence ever so slightly. Consequently, I took it to a whole new level. But I should've known better.

"And that X and O were for real," I said in my best seductress voice—not that I've practiced. But then I stepped closer to him. So close that I could smell his cologne, or maybe it was just him, but the scent was somewhat intoxicating. Jason is only a couple of inches taller than me, and I was looking straight into his eyes. The next thing I knew we were kissing. First in a tentative way and then with passion. And suddenly everything was spinning and blurry, and I thought I could feel my feet lifting off the ground.

"Jason!" yelled one of the other guys on the crew. "Get your butt over here now!"

Jason immediately let go of me and stepped back. "Sorry, Maya, I shouldn't have done that."

"No, it's okay. I wanted—"

"I gotta get to work." And then he dashed off.

Well, I was still floating as I went back to my room to day-dream for a while. And I was still walking on air that evening on my way to the concert, not to listen to my dad, but hoping to simply catch a glimpse of Jason. I rode down on the elevator and was actually dreaming of the next time Jason and I would be together, maybe even later that evening. And as I entered the lobby, I was imagining what our wedding would be like and how many children we'd have, and suddenly, like the popping of a balloon, I heard my dad calling my name from the other side of the lobby. He was dressed for the concert, but his expression did not look even slightly entertaining. I hurried over to see what was wrong.

"I had to let Jason go," he sternly informed me.

"What—why?" I asked, although I was pretty sure I knew the answer.

"Ham said he saw you two backstage earlier today, Maya, acting in an inappropriate way."

I didn't respond, just looked down at the carpet as a mixed-up mess of feelings rushed through me.

"I confronted Jason, and he didn't deny it."

I looked back up now. "And you fired him?"

"In his defense, he had no idea you were only sixteen. He was pretty shocked when I told him that."

"But I'm old for my age."

"Sixteen is still sixteen."

I could feel tears coming now. "You really fired him?"

"I told him to pack his bags and collect his check from Thomas."

"But, Dad—"

"No buts, Maya. Jason is gone. I'll give him my recommendation, but he is off the show." Dad shook his head. "And we need to come up with another plan for you too."

I frowned. "For me?"

He softened slightly. "You are way too beautiful and too young to be hanging around a bunch of crusty old dudes. Thomas warned me right from the get-go that having you on tour was a formula for disaster, but I didn't believe him. Jason was the first one to cave."

"But Jason's not like those other guys. Jason is different. And it's not even his fault—"

"Let it go, Maya!" Dad's face grew stormy. "Jason is gone, and I don't have time to discuss this with you at the moment." He glanced at his watch. "I just wanted you to know what was up."

So I went to my room, and I haven't spoken to Dad since then. I am mad and brokenhearted and totally frustrated. It's like the whole universe is set against me. Sometimes I wonder why I don't just give up... Why do I even keep trying?

Maya's Green Tip for the Day

Did you know that a full bus is six times more fuel efficient than a car with just one passenger? And a full rail car is fifteen times more efficient. And right now I'm thinking of jumping the next train!

Fifteen

February 20

Dad and I have both been doing a silent act this week. Well, his isn't a completely silent act since he still talks to the crew, but not to me. And I speak to no one. I'm well aware that I'm acting like a juvenile. But according to my dad, that's what I am. So why not just play it out? Who really gives a rip anyway?

It was Dad who finally ended the silent war. He took me aside today, giving me a look that suggested I'd better listen.

"I talked to Shannon this morning."

I didn't say a word, just shrugged. The truth of the matter was that I had also spoken to Shannon earlier this week. According to her, she was still clean and sober, but she was also slightly depressed, which is never a good sign. "I have nothing, Maya," she told me in a dramatic tone. "Just an empty shell of a life. No family, no career. The pitiful truth is that I have hardly any friends. Not real ones anyway. I think I know the difference now."

"What about Myrna?"

"I think I'm more Myrna's project than a friend."

I didn't say so, but I could imagine that.

"How long do you plan to stay with your father, Maya?"

"I don't know…"

This was followed by a long, uncomfortable silence. I almost thought she'd hung up. And so, knowing it wasn't smart, I actually confided in her. Call me crazy or just plain desperate, I told her all about Jason and how Dad had fired him and how it was so unfair.

And she actually laughed, which just made me downright furious.

"Sorry I even told you," I said in my snippiest voice, realizing how stupid I'd been to tell her.

"No no…," she said quickly. "You don't get it, Maya. I wasn't laughing at you and Jason. I was just laughing at how ironic that is. Do you have any idea how old I was when your dad and I first started dating? Or for that matter, how old he was?"

"No…"

"I was a ripe old seventeen, and your father was twenty-seven, or so he said. Later on I found out he was two years older than that."

"No way."

She laughed even louder now, and her voice sounded

genuinely happy...or almost. "Yes. I can't believe he's acting like such an old fuddy-duddy."

"Well, I am his daughter, and he's been trying to be a good dad." Suddenly I felt bad for how I'd been treating him and for reporting on him. I mean, in all fairness his track record outshines Shannon's. And there I had been bad-mouthing him. What kind of daughter am I?

That was probably one of the main reasons I softened up when he broke the silence today. Guilt—it's like a magic potion.

"Anyway," Dad continued slowly, like he was weighing each word and not totally sure of himself, "Shannon seems to be committed to her sobriety, Maya."

I couldn't help rolling my eyes. I mean, yes, she seems to be committed, and I certainly wish her the best and hope that it's the real thing, but if history is supposed to be the best indicator of the future...well, just imagine.

"I know...I know...," he said. "Shannon could be falling off the wagon right now, but I'd like to think she's not. Wouldn't you?"

"Duh." Okay, that wasn't exactly a mature response, but as I mentioned, I have not been feeling particularly grown-up recently.

"Anyway...since we're nearby,"—we were in Las Vegas once again—"well, I thought maybe you'd want to pay your mom a little visit. Just to see how she's doing."

"Meaning that you're dumping me with her?"

"No, I'm not dumping you, sweetheart. But for your sake, I simply want to come up with a better plan for you than living on the road with a bunch of funky old guys."

"Sorry to complicate your life."

He put his hand on my cheek. "That's not the case, and you know it, Maya. But somebody's got to make the money to pay the bills."

I shrugged. "Money can be highly overrated."

"I remember a time not so long ago when you were flipping-out mad at Shannon for stealing your money."

I brightened now. "And if you'd like to replace that money, maybe I could continue to file for emancipation like I'd planned to do."

He frowned. "I just can't see how that's in your best interest, Maya."

"What is in my best interest?"

"An education, for one thing. Thomas was looking into boarding schools, and I thought—"

"Boarding schools?" I stared indignantly at him. "Are you serious?"

"He says there are some good ones back east."

"I am not going to be locked up in a stupid boarding school."

He sighed. "Yes…it's hard to imagine you restricted like that. You've had a lot of freedom."

"Fine! I'll go back to Shannon."

"You will?"

"And I'll go back to modeling. And I'll put my money in an account with only my name on it. And I swear to you I will be emancipated by summer."

He didn't seem too pleased to hear this but simply nodded. "Then it's settled."

I still felt angry at him. And betrayed. "Yes. It's settled."

And so it is that I feel like a yo-yo or a Ping-Pong ball or maybe just a bad penny... I wonder how many times I'll have to bounce back and forth between them before I'm free. But my flight has been booked, and I'll be back with Shannon by tomorrow evening. Whoopee.

March 11

"This is Day Seventy-three," Shannon announced as she held up her coffee mug in a mock toast. It was her usual morning ritual. And I must admit it was getting a wee bit old after almost three weeks. Still, I smiled and reminded myself that there were worse things. Far worse.

"Any big shoots today?" she asked.

"Actually, I do have one callback today, not that it means much." It hadn't been easy getting back into the swing of things. While Ms. Montgomery seemed glad to have me back, I had earned a bit of a reputation thanks to my quick departure in December.

"No one wants to hire a flaky model," Campbell had told me shortly after I got back. "No matter how pretty she is."

I considered explaining myself but couldn't think of anything believable to say. So I didn't. Still, it's been slow going with only one real shoot, and it didn't pay much. But hopefully that was about to turn around. On the bright side, Shannon had been behaving herself. Although I could tell she was bored.

"I need something to do," she had complained last night.

"Want to help with my garden?" I suggested. I think this was rather generous on my part since I'm very territorial when it comes to my garden. But it had been so neglected during my absence that I knew it was going to take a lot of work to get it back. Maybe a little weeding would do Shannon some good.

But she simply sat at the table studying her nails. "I don't think so... I just got a manicure on Monday."

"What about acting?" I asked. Okay, I know this is almost an invitation for trouble since Shannon can get upset when she remembers what she gave up (yeah, right) for me and my dad.

"No one wants an old lady."

"There are lots of parts for older women," I said. Then to take the sting out, I reminded her of all the amazing actresses who are older than she is. "Goldie Hawn, Meryl Streep, Jane

Seymour, Susan Sarandon, Diane Keaton...just to name a few."

She brightened now. "Yes...maybe you're right, Maya. Maybe it's time to accept that I'm getting older. And maybe it's time to speak to my agent."

"You have an agent?"

She frowned. "Well, my old agent. He's still around."

March 14

As it turns out, this hasn't been a great week for either of us. Shannon's agent politely but bluntly told her he wasn't interested. And my callback opportunity, the people I'd been hoping would offer a contract, changed their minds. "They decided that they need a blonde," the photographer's assistant informed me. Never mind that I'd spent two hours getting ready, paid for a taxi, and sat and waited for an hour to hear their good news.

But that's not the worst part of my life. The scariest development is that I'm afraid Shannon has fallen off the wagon again. No, I don't think she's doing drugs, not yet anyway. But after her "crushing" disappointment about her acting career, she met an old friend "for drinks." It figured that she would call someone like Lynnette, since she's also an out-of-work actor with addiction problems of her own. Although the last I heard, Lynnette had been clean for quite some time. It's possible I'm overreacting. Still, something about it doesn't smell right.

"But you're in rehab," I reminded Shannon after I smelled booze on her breath. "And you've been doing so well. Why risk everything now?"

"First of all, this is not drugs, Maya. It was a couple of beers, a little pick-me-up with an old friend. I didn't even have the hard stuff. So just cut me some slack, and chill, *girlfriend.*"

I hate when she calls me "girlfriend."

And this afternoon when I got back from another exhausting day of dropping off tear sheets and trying to look pretty, dependable, and not desperate, Shannon was gone. It was only around five o'clock, so I told myself that she might be out shopping. Since she's been paying her bills (actually just making minimum payments on her charge cards), she has a little bit of credit available. So I was hoping that was the case. But now it's close to midnight, and she still isn't home...not a good sign.

Mostly I just hope she's not out there doing something really, really stupid. If she's using again, I will be so out of here. I don't even care where I go. I just refuse to live like that again.

Maya's Green Tip for the Day

Did you know that between 500 billion and a trillion plastic grocery bags are used on this planet each year? That's a lot of plastic. And even if you've switched to a reusable shopping bag, you may still have a lot of plastic bags in your house. There are some interesting ways to put these bags to a second-time use. You can cut the plastic into strips to create "plastic yarn." And if you know how to knit or crochet, you can make all kinds of things—everything from dog leashes to belts to rugs to purses. It's only as limited as your imagination. Why not go online and see if you can find some new ideas for recycling plastic bags? Or as I've mentioned, you can at least recycle them as trash bags or return them to the grocery store. It doesn't take a genius to do that.

Sixteen

March 18

I'm not sure whether to be relieved or worried today. I don't even know where to begin with this latest development in the life of Maya Stark, but I'm starting to wonder if my journal couldn't be a good documentary about what happens to kids who are "raised" by psychotic parents. Anne Frank I am not. But I do have a story that deserves to be heard. And since my modeling career is taking some time to jump-start, maybe I should consider turning my journal into a screenplay. I wonder where I could find a fifty-something Britney Spears kind of actor. Or perhaps Shannon could play herself. She's such a natural at it.

Okay, all kidding aside, I had to take Shannon to the emergency room about one o'clock this morning. She and Lynnette had gone out to celebrate Saint Patrick's Day.

"We jus' wanted to drink some green beer," Shannon slurred at me after I found her flat on her back at the foot of the stairs. I'd been sound asleep when I'd awakened to a crash and a scream, and certain that burglars were in the house, I grabbed my cell phone and called 911.

"What is the nature of your emergency?" asked a calm man on the other end.

"I think maybe a break-in," I whispered as I peered out the crack of my door.

"How many people are in the house?"

Just then I saw one of Shannon's shoes—a silly pair of pink sandals with about four-inch heels. "Never mind," I said quickly.

Of course, he wasn't about to let me off the hook, so I explained what had happened. "It's just my mom," I said with disgust. "She fell down."

"Does she need assistance?"

Just the men in white coats with a straitjacket, I wanted to tell him. "No..." I looked down at Shannon to see that her eyes were wide open and she had a goofy-looking smile. Obviously wasted. She held up her hand and gave me a little finger wave. "I'm sorry to bother you, sir," I said calmly.

"Just so you know, an officer is already en route."

"Why?"

"It's just routine. He'll make sure that everything is okay."

"But everything *is* okay," I said. The last thing I wanted was the police to find my intoxicated mom acting like an imbecile. But before I could think of a way out, I saw lights outside the front door, and then someone was knocking.

"I'm sorry," I told the officer at the front door. "I thought someone had broken in, but it was just my mom. She knocked a picture off the wall, and it made a big noise, and—"

"I'll just have a quick look around and make sure you're okay," he said in a friendly tone. Still, as he came in the house, his hand was near his gun—like what did he think was going on here?

Shannon was sitting on the bottom step now, rubbing her right foot and frowning.

"Everything okay in here, ma'am?" He peered down at her curiously.

"I think I broke something," she said without even blinking. Did she not think it strange that a policeman was in our house?

He stooped down to look at her foot. "It's sure swollen, ma'am. Did you fall?"

I wanted to point out that she was falling-down drunk, but I simply put the knocked-down picture back on the wall and stared at my mom.

"I sort of tripped on the stairs. I can't exactly remember. Maybe I hit my head."

"Do you want me to call for medical transport?" he offered.

"No," I said quickly. "I mean, we don't have very good insurance coverage right now. If she needs to go to the hospital, I can take her."

"You're a driver?"

I nodded. "And I've heard how outrageously expensive an ambulance ride can be," I said, hoping to create a smoke screen. Surely this guy wasn't going to demand to see my driver's license—the one I still didn't have.

"You're right about that."

"My daughter will take care of me," Shannon said. I think the realization was sinking in. Perhaps having a policeman here to witness her being wasted with only a minor daughter to handle things might not look good. "We'll just put some ice on it." She rubbed her foot. "Probably be fine in the morning."

"Okay…then I'll be on my way." He smiled at both of us. "You girls take care now."

But as soon as he was gone, Shannon began bawling. "Take me to the hospital." Saying it over and over until I wanted to slap her. Instead I went and got some ice.

"You said you could wait until morning."

"I can't," she wailed. "I think it's broken. It hurts."

And so I somehow managed to get her into the car, and I drove us to the hospital. And as it turned out, her foot was broken.

"See, I told you," she proclaimed proudly as they helped me wheel her out to the car around seven this morning. She had a cast on, a pair of crutches, and some pain pills. I was surprised they didn't give her a lollipop too since she was acting like a child.

Anyway, I finally got her settled into a downstairs bedroom and brought her some breakfast and coffee, which she insisted she needed but barely touched. And now she is sleeping it off.

So the good news is that she's going to be stuck at home with a broken foot for a while. The bad news is that she called Lynnette from the hospital, and after Lynnette heard the news, she offered to come over here to help out. But I suspect that Lynnette is here to help herself out. She mentioned that her rent's overdue and she's been looking for a new place to stay. I'm afraid she may have picked us.

But maybe the bright side is that this will free me up to get jobs and hopefully start earning some money. Although Shannon has promised to pay me back my money, I don't have any great hopes that this will happen soon. If I'm going to break out of this joint, it's probably going to have to be on my own dime.

March 29

It's gone from bad to worse...and why am I surprised? It started with Shannon's pain pills. She ran out way too soon. That's when Lynnette stepped in. And when I checked out. I'd been getting jobs the past week, and I'd put my first good-sized check into my own checking and savings account. An account I opened at a completely different bank. An account that I will protect from Shannon. Especially now, since I can see where she is heading.

Take last night, for instance. Despite the fact that Shannon is still on crutches, she and Lynnette went out partying. And Shannon drove—cast and all. As it turned out, they were stopped by the police on their way home. Naturally, Shannon was arrested for DUI and was treated to a free night in jail. Her car was impounded, and somehow— I still don't know how and don't want to know—Lynnette scraped together enough money to bail Shannon out this afternoon. Of course they both called me, begging for financial help. I declined. As of today, I am not speaking to either of them. And I have threatened to call my dad, but he's performing in Jamaica at the moment, and I know it would be a major inconvenience to have to come here.

I've decided that Lynnette is a parasite. Or worse. Besides leading Shannon back into the bar world, she might be bringing drugs into this house. Okay, I suppose it's possible I'm just extremely paranoid, but I don't think so. Mostly I keep to myself and hope that I can get enough money to make my exit in a couple of months. Ms. Montgomery said that things are starting to pick up again and that spring is usually a busy time for models. I can only hope.

April 4

The situation has become desperate. I came home from a photo shoot late this afternoon to find that Shannon and Lynnette are having a party tonight. A party?! Shannon is barely out of jail, her car is still impounded, and she's been too broke to buy groceries this week. I actually loaned her forty bucks for food yesterday.

"How can you afford a party?" I asked when I found the two in the kitchen with not only a bunch of junky-looking food but booze as well. And although it looked like a pile of crap, I could tell it was expensive.

Shannon just smiled mysteriously.

"Big Daddy," said Lynnette. Then Shannon gave her a sharp elbow.

"My dad sent money? Some of that is for me, you know!"

"Don't worry," said Shannon.

"Yes, it takes money to make money," added Lynnette.

"What?"

But Shannon shushed her, and feeling like I wanted to hit someone or maybe two someones, I just took off. I went to my room and gathered up my things and considered running away. But where? I have a photo shoot tomorrow at one, and I can't risk missing it. Especially if things continue to spiral downward on the home front.

Finally I decided just to sneak my stuff as well as some provisions up to the attic. At least I won't be stuck downstairs if the party gets really out of hand, which I'm guessing could happen. And somehow I will make a plan to get out of here by next week. Maybe Myrna would like to adopt me for a couple of months.

Later the same awful night...

News flash: Shannon Stark's party has been busted! Okay, I keep telling myself that I should be partially relieved since this will absolutely put a stop to the craziness. But it's just been so weird. And I have to admit...scary.

Naturally, I started to freak when I saw flashing lights below. I actually thought maybe the house was on fire. Then I looked out the window to see five or six cop cars pulling into the driveway. And I thought maybe this would teach Shannon a lesson.

But when the police entered the house, it got really loud down there—everyone was screaming and running, like it was a real raid. And I could hear the cops yelling and telling everyone to get down on the ground and stuff like that. I was hoping no one would start shooting.

Consequently, I remained up here the whole time. I felt like a mouse in the attic, just waiting until it all settled down. I quietly positioned myself by the window so I could see when the cops left, waiting for the coast to clear. But that didn't happen right away. After the initial bust, things quieted

down. Then it got noisy again with doors opening and closing, like someone was going through every closet and cabi-
net and whatever. The cops were probably doing a very
thorough search of our house. And who knew what they
might have found.

Thankfully they didn't come up to the attic. But it was
really unnerving. And I was tempted to call my dad and
beg him to send someone out to get me. However, he's just
started his European tour, and he's going to be hard to
reach for a while. Besides, I kept telling myself that I could
deal with this.

Finally it's around three in the morning, and most of the
partiers have either left the house or been taken away in cop
cars. Now there are only three cars left, and I think the "party"
is almost over. But then Shannon is escorted out the front
door by a woman cop. Shannon still has on her short denim
skirt and a pink tank top, only now her outfit is accented with
a pair of handcuffs. The cop helps my mom into the back of a
patrol car, then slams the door.

I know it makes no sense, but I feel really sad, and my
hands begin to shake. I pick up my cell phone, thinking I will
call someone, but who? Earlier tonight when I was feeling
frustrated and lonely, I actually e-mailed my cousin Kim and
confessed all, although I'm sort of regretting that. But there
is no way I'm calling her now. Not at this time of night. Also,

I notice that my cell phone battery is almost dead, and I didn't bring the charger. So I just wait. I wait and feel freaked. I try not to think about what I'm going to do. Where I'll go if Shannon is in any kind of serious trouble. And for all I know, she could be. I do know this: I don't have any bail money.

Not too long after Shannon's escorted out of the house, the other cops get into their cars, taking various other guests from the party along with them—not anyone I recognize, not that I expected to. I haven't seen Lynnette exiting yet, and I wonder if she made a fast break earlier.

At last the house becomes very quiet. Still, I'm not sure I want to go down there, not until daylight anyway. I try to sleep, but it's like the adrenaline keeps rushing through me. My hands are shaking so badly that I almost wonder if Shannon hid some of her stupid amphetamines or something in my water bottle.

Okay, I know that's ridiculous, but it's like I can't stop shaking. I feel like I'm having a meltdown. And it's impossible to sleep. Finally the sun comes up, and I think it should be safe to leave. So I pack up my stuff and am about to go down when I hear someone in the house!

I look out to see if there's a car but don't see one. Still, someone is definitely in the house. And they are definitely searching for something. It can't be anything good. And I don't think it's the police. So who does that leave? Some whacked-out crackhead with a gun? Okay, now I am totally freaked, and my brain is fried from all this stress. So I just stay in the attic, getting a serious case of claustrophobia—it feels like I can't breathe. I'm afraid to move, and I can't open the window. I think I'm going to die.

Seventeen

April 7

The past two days have been a blur…surreal. My cousin Kim not only e-mailed me back on that horrid night, telling me to get out of that house, which I eventually did, but my uncle decided I should come out and spend some time with them. I didn't argue.

And yesterday I got on a flight (which Uncle Allen paid for), and he and Kim picked me up at the airport. I'm sure they expected more gratitude from me, but the truth is, I feel dead inside. It's like something in me is broken, and I don't think it's ever going to be fixed.

Kim showed me to the guest room. I only brought one bag, the same backpack that I threw things into on Friday night. I was too rattled and scared when I finally made my break out of the house midday Saturday. I wasn't even sure if I was going to make it. It seemed that people had been coming and going all morning. Strangers, I think. Then the police. And finally Lynnette was down there yelling for me. I never answered. I don't even know why. Except that I wanted out of there. For good. Naturally, I missed my photo shoot. My modeling career is over now. I do not care.

After settling into "my" room, I slept the rest of the day. And when I spoke with Kim that evening, I didn't say much. I know she thinks I'm a snob or a brat or just a pathetic loser whose parents should never have been allowed to have kids.

"I spoke to your dad's manager," my uncle informed me last night. "Your dad should be calling you tomorrow around ten. I told him it was fine to call on the house phone."

And my dad does call this morning. I am the only one home at the time. Kim had school. My uncle had work. It is a relief to be able to speak candidly, which I do. I pour out the whole ugly story.

"But you're okay?" my dad finally asks.

"Yeah. I'm great."

"You don't sound great."

I know I've been speaking in a monotone. But what do people expect? I wonder if this is sort of how a soldier feels after coming home from war. Shell shock? Is that what they call it?

"What do you want me to do, Maya?"

I consider this. But I can't tell him my true answer. I can't say, "I want you to come home and act like you're my dad. I want you to take care of me. I want you to love me and get us a home where we can live like normal people. Like Kim and her dad." Yeah, right. Like that's going to happen. "I don't know," I finally mutter.

"Well, I've been thinking about your emancipation idea," he says. "And I'm willing to sign off for you."

Now I know this should make me glad. It's what I wanted. But instead, I feel a hard lump in my throat.

"And Shannon will have no choice but to sign off for you, Maya."

"Right..."

"And I want to replace what she stole from you, and more. If you'll give me your account number, I'll have Thomas set that up. And I'll have him do a direct deposit into your account each month so you'll have your own money to live on. I should've done that a long time ago. Sorry."

I let out a long sigh. "Yeah."

"Are you going to be okay, baby?"

"I'm fine." I feel tears slipping out now.

"I talked to Allen. He seems like a really nice guy. And his daughter sounds like she has a good head on her shoulders too. I think you're in good hands."

"Yeah."

"And I'll be back in the States the end of May. Maybe we can figure something out then, something more permanent."

"Right..."

"In the meantime you can e-mail me. It's hard catching calls over here with the time difference and all."

I don't point out that he hardly ever checks his e-mail. Why bother?

"You're a survivor, Maya," he says in his you-can-do-anything voice. "You're going to come out on top, baby. I just know it."

We say a few more things. Or he says a few more things, finally promising to find out what's going on with Shannon, when he has time, that is. And then we hang up, and I go back to the guest room and have a good, long cry.

April 11

"Why don't you just stay here?" Kim said after she got home from school yesterday. I'd been telling her and my uncle that I needed to make a plan and that I needed to get out of here and get on with my life. But at that moment, I wasn't sure if I could even get off their sofa without help. I felt paralyzed.

"And do what?" I frowned up at her. As usual, she looked like a fashion-conscious preppy—nice and neat with her sleek black hair cut into layers that frame her serious dark eyes and petite facial features. I think Kim is really pretty, and if she were about a foot taller, she could probably even model. Not that she would. She's too smart to get caught up in something like that.

"Go to school. Make friends. Live your life." She smiled with satisfaction, as if—just like that—she'd put my messed-up world into perfect order.

I just stared at her in disbelief. It was like someone from a different planet had said, "Hey, let's fly on over to Jupiter and eat a live octopus for lunch." I mean, I couldn't even wrap my mind around it.

Kim sat down next to me and actually put a hand on my shoulder. And just that small act of kindness was enough to break me down. So I pulled away. But that didn't stop her. "Look, Maya, I know you've been through a lot. Probably more than anyone realizes. But that doesn't mean you can't have a normal life now…if you want one."

"I don't even know what normal is." Of course, I didn't admit to her that normal is what I've been wanting for ages now. Or that I'd given up on ever finding it for myself.

"Well, there probably is no real normal," she said. "It's more like an illusion. Or maybe it's whatever you decide to make it. But I do believe you can have a life that's different… healthier…than the one you've been living."

"I don't know…"

"Are you open to advice?"

I considered this, then shrugged.

"Why don't you enroll at my high school? Just give it a try. There are only two months left in the school year, but it might be enough time for you to figure things out."

"You want me to stick around for two months?" I studied her reaction closely. I mean, I know she's a Christian...and I wondered if this was just some goody-goody-girl act. But I have to admit she seemed sincere.

"Two months will probably go by pretty quickly," she said. "But you might discover that you like it here."

I think I frowned then.

"Or you might not like it." She grinned. "But at least you'd know."

"That's not it," I admitted. "I don't want to feel like you have to drag me around, like it's your job to help me figure things out. And just for the record, I need you to understand that I'm a very independent person."

She actually laughed then. "I already knew that."

"Oh..."

"And *just for the record,* I'm a very busy person. So unless you specifically want me to help you with something, I'll assume you can handle stuff yourself."

"Thanks."

"But if you'd like, I could give you a ride to school tomorrow. And I could point you in the direction of the office. But that would be it."

"I'll think about it."

"Cool. Maybe you could let me know what you decide."

And so I decided. Or sort of. Anyway, I did go to school

with Kim today. And I met with a guidance counselor. I started by telling her that I'd been doing homeschool and that my school records might be a little messed up.

Mrs. King gave me a curious look. "So what grade would you say you're in now?"

"I already have my GED."

"You have your GED?" She blinked.

Finally I decided to just spill the beans. Seriously, what could it hurt? Besides, if she's a good counselor, she should be understanding, right? As expected, she was surprised and impressed to learn that I'm Nick Stark's daughter.

"Not that I want everyone to know," I said quickly.

"Yes, I can understand that."

So then I told her about my mom. And even the news I'd just heard, via my dad, that she will probably be doing time in the L.A. jail for drug possession and sales, among other things.

"Wow," Mrs. King said after I finished, "you've certainly been through a lot, Maya."

I nodded. "And I plan to go ahead with the emancipation. My dad has agreed, and, well, my mom doesn't really have a say now. But...I don't know...I thought it might be interesting to see how I like high school. My cousin Kim Peterson thinks I should give it a try."

"Kim Peterson is your cousin?"

So I explained how our moms were estranged sisters and how, thanks to my mom's messed-up life, I'm living with Kim and her dad for the time being.

"Kim is a wonderful girl," said Mrs. King. Then she handed me some paperwork. "Do the best you can to fill these out, and if you don't mind, I'll set up some placement testing for you on Monday."

"Placement testing?"

"Well, although you have your GED, it doesn't tell us much about what academics you may be lacking. And come to think of it, it might not be too late to get you signed up for pre-SATs."

"Pre-SATs?"

"Our college-bound juniors take the test to see what they need to study further during their senior year."

I didn't point out that if I'd been going to school like a normal teen, I wouldn't even be a junior yet. Really, what difference would it make anyway? I simply filled out the paperwork and agreed to show up on Monday for my placement testing.

"How hard is it to get a driver's license in your state?" I asked as Kim drove us home. Her friend Natalie, also a senior, was in the front seat. I don't like to make snap judgments about people, but I didn't like Natalie much from the get-go. It wasn't just her fashion obsessions and styled-within-an-inch-of-its-life blond hair as much as it was her voice and her opinions. To be honest, I wasn't even sure why she and Kim were friends. But as usual, I kept these thoughts to myself.

"Do you have your learner's permit?" asked Natalie.

"No, but I know how to drive."

Kim laughed. "That's not going to impress the DMV."

"Probably not."

So they explained the steps, and Kim even swung by the DMV to get some booklets and things. Of course, this brought up the need for emancipation again. So I realized I had some work to do.

"What do you think of Harrison High?" Natalie asked as we all got back into Kim's Jeep Wrangler.

"I don't know," I said. "It seems kind of small."

"Compared to *Beverly Hills*?" Natalie said in a weird tone. Like she was making fun of where I lived. I decided to let it go.

"Maya was homeschooled," Kim said quietly.

"Seriously?" Natalie turned and stared at me like I was an alien. "Wow, you just don't seem like the homeschooled type to me."

"And that would be what?" Okay, I knew I sounded snooty, but I didn't care. This girl gets on my nerves. It's like she has a superiority complex. And then I was thinking, *Isn't this the girl who got pregnant last year?* Not that I'm going there. I am not.

"Oh, you know," Natalie said lightly, "homeschooled kids are usually in really strict Christian homes and—"

"That seems like a narrow perspective," I pointed out.

"That's right," agreed Kim. "People from all walks of life do homeschooling, Nat."

Well, that shut Natalie up. And after we got home, I wasted no time in getting away from them. Rather, from Natalie. Still, it made me wonder. What am I getting into here? This is a small town where normal actually exists, or so it seems. Girls like me don't really fit in. And yet in some ways, this small-town life feels like a break. Like I can almost breathe again. Almost.

April 18

I've just finished my first week in a real high school. Pretty weird. But sort of cool too. After my testing, which seemed to impress Mrs. King, she asked if I wanted to be placed as a junior this year.

"Meaning I would be a senior next year?"

She smiled. "It seems that way."

This was actually a huge relief. I'd been worried that I was going to be like a freshman, with three more years until graduation. And if that was the case, I was considering just going with the GED and calling it a day.

"That sounds good," I told her. "Well, if I decide I like school."

She nodded. "Let's hope you do. You're a very smart girl, Maya. And I think you'd have a good chance for some scholarships." Then she looked uneasy. "Not that you'd need them...I mean, with your father and all."

"Don't forget about my emancipation," I reminded her.

"Yes...of course."

"Although my dad is helping me out financially." Not that I can totally count on that. The bottom could fall out for him on any given day. His career bombed once. I'm sure it could happen again. Besides, if I'm going to make it in this world, I'll probably need to make it on my own.

"I heard you didn't bring much with you from California, Maya," Natalie said as Kim drove us home from school. "Maybe you'd like us to take you shopping."

"Shopping?"

"You know, for some clothes and things."

"It may come as a surprise to you," I said in a sharp tone, "but some of us are not that into shopping."

"Oh," Natalie said. "Is it like that vegan thing? You don't eat meat or wear leather, and you don't like new clothes either?"

I was starting to fume now, and I tried not to think of how I compromised myself by wearing leather to work...and for modeling. Not that it did me any good.

"Unlike some people, Maya isn't a slave to fashion," Kim said.

Yay, Kim!

"Meaning you think *I'm* a slave to fashion?" Natalie asked in a shocked tone.

"Not as much as you used to be," Kim said. "But you have to admit, you've been known to shop—"

"Just because I care about my appearance doesn't mean I'm a slave to fashion!"

Suddenly, and to my relief, they were the ones arguing. Okay, I felt a teeny twinge of guilt, but mostly I was glad the spotlight was off me.

Maya's Green Tip for the Day

Sometimes you'll see the words "organic cotton" on a T-shirt. Do you know what this means? It doesn't have anything to do with the quality of cotton, since cotton is basically cotton. It has to do with how the cotton is raised. Instead of using chemicals that can harm the land and waterways, organic cotton growers use natural pesticides and fertilizers. So if you pay a little more to purchase organic cotton, you're helping keep the planet safer.

Eighteen

April 21

I got my learner's permit today, thanks to the help of Uncle Allen (that's what he said to call him). And it's hard not to like the guy. He's got this receding hairline and gray hair and a slight paunch and glasses, but these features only make me like him more. In fact, weird as it sounds, he reminds me of my favorite overalls. Nicely worn and comfortable.

Anyway, Uncle Allen somehow managed to coordinate, between his attorney and my dad, getting a form of temporary guardianship over me. This is only until my emancipation is complete. And according to Uncle Allen's attorney, that shouldn't take long. Kim has made it clear that she doesn't really approve of my plans, not that she's making it difficult for me. I also sense that Uncle Allen has questions. But fortunately, he keeps them to himself.

"Thanks," I told him as he drove home from the DMV. "I really appreciate you taking time off work to do this for me."

"I was glad to help, Maya."

"The only problem now…," I said with some uncertainty, "is that I need to accumulate fifty hours of driving time with someone over the age of twenty-one. And ten of those hours need to be night driving."

"I'm over twenty-one," he said, "and I've been through all this before, with Kim. Patricia…your aunt…preferred me teaching Kim to drive."

"I already know how to drive," I said.

"Really?" And suddenly he was turning onto a side street. Then he got out of the car and opened my door. "Go for it."

"Seriously?"

"Sure, why not? Show me what you got."

So I drove us home, and when I got there, he seemed pleased. "You really do know how to drive. Who taught you?"

"No one."

He looked curious. "No one?"

So I explained about Shannon's need for chauffeuring from time to time. "I had to learn."

"Looks like this will be easy then."

"You mean other than the fifty hours?"

"Well, maybe you and Kim and I can do some road trips. We could show you the sights, such as they are."

"That'd be great. And I've already signed up for driver's ed, although it doesn't start until June. But my goal is to be driving by summer." I didn't tell him that I'd also be looking for a job and another place to live. My plan is to be on my own by the time Kim leaves for college in August. I'm pretty sure that's what Uncle Allen would prefer too.

April 24

After not even two weeks in this town, I am almost starting to feel as if I might fit in. Or sort of. Although I'm not sure that's what Uncle Allen or Kim is thinking, because the truth is, I keep an extremely low profile in their home. I don't leave any messes. And for the most part I take care of my own food, which they seem to respect since neither of them gets the vegan thing. I do my own laundry, and I even started working in the garden out back, which seemed to please my uncle. So really, it's almost as if I'm not here. Or so I like to think. Mostly I don't want to wear out my welcome. At least not before I get the whole emancipation thing settled and get my driver's license in hand. Then I can take the next step.

And for sure I don't mean to suggest that I fit in at Harrison High. It's not like everyone there has accepted me and I'll be voted prom queen or anything lame like that. Not that my misfit complex has to do with ethnicity. I mean, the school doesn't have a ton of diversity, but there's definitely a mix. But I feel like an oddity because of my background. In this small town I doubt that many teens have parents doing time for drugs. But I could be wrong.

Still, I'm surprised to find that I'm starting to relax a little. And some people at school are even talking to me now.

It seems that some of them actually want to get to know me. Not that I'm jumping into anything. Lately I've been eating lunch with Marissa, a senior in my art class, and her friends. I almost feel like I fit in with them. And one of these guys, Jake, seems to be putting the move on me. Not that I care.

But then as I'm beginning to feel somewhat comfortable, I'm shocked to discover that sometimes Kim and Natalie eat lunch with these kids too. Okay, I'm more surprised about Nat than Kim. Although Marissa told me that is due to Chloe Miller, a girl who went to school here but graduated early to play in her Christian rock band. Apparently she befriended both Marissa and Kim.

"Christian rock band?" I questioned. "Sounds like an oxymoron or something."

Marissa laughed. "Yeah, it sounds weird. But when you meet Chloe, you'll get it. She's totally cool. And so is Kim. It's just Natalie who takes some getting used to."

And I have to agree with her there. Mostly I try not to engage with Kim's best friend. But for some reason, Natalie seems to have set her sights on me. Like today.

"I hope you know that Spencer is into drugs," Natalie warned me as Kim drove us home from school today. I knew she was saying this because she'd seen me hanging with Marissa and Spencer in the parking lot after school. And probably because she saw them both smoking cigarettes.

Like, *Oh, no, they were smoking. That probably means they're taking drugs too.*

Seriously, it's like she wants to have this off-the-wall running commentary on my life. Like she thinks I need someone like her to help me find my way. Sometimes I try to humor her, but sometimes she just makes it difficult.

"I know you're new," she continued, "and you're probably not aware that Spencer has a history, but I feel it only fair to warn you."

Meaning no one else has a history? I wanted to ask but didn't. I hate it when anyone, especially Natalie, treats me like I'm a child. Even though she's older than me and about to graduate. And then it occurred to me that she's got some history too. She's had some experiences that I haven't (like getting pregnant, getting married, having a baby—the kinds of experiences I would just as soon put off for about twenty years), but surely that doesn't give her the right to act like she is so much more mature than I am. I think that's what bugs me most about her.

As usual, I ignored her.

"Spencer's not a bad guy," said Kim defensively. "Not really. He's just a little misdirected."

Misdirected? What was that supposed to mean? Like the sign said turn left, and he'd turned right?

"Meaning he needs God in his life," Natalie stated with authority. Like she had the secret remedy, like if we all just listened to her and inserted God in our lives, we'd be just fine. That would solve everything. Tell me another.

"So what makes you such an expert on what other people need?" I asked, then instantly regretted it.

"It says in the Bible that we all need God."

"Not everyone believes in the Bible."

"Just because they don't believe in something doesn't mean it's not the truth," she tossed back. "Like people used to believe the world was flat, but now we know they were wrong."

"Do you know this for a fact? Have you been around the world to see whether it's really round or flat? Or do you simply believe what you read or what someone told you?"

Kim laughed.

"That's ridiculous," Natalie said, unruffled. "*Everyone* knows that—"

"You seem to enjoy speaking for *everyone*," I retorted.

"I just enjoy speaking the truth," she said. "I have strong convictions, and I don't care who hears them. It's all part of being a Christian."

Okay, I know it was stupid, but I just couldn't control myself. Besides, from what Marissa had told me, Natalie's tarnished reputation is common knowledge anyway. "So can I assume that your Christian convictions endorse premarital sex? Because I must admit, that's a new one to me."

Kim's eyebrows shot up, and I knew that was a warning for me to stop, but it was too late. The elephant was in the living room, and far be it from me to pretend that it wasn't.

"Not that I've known all that many Christians," I continued, "but the ones I knew were a little uptight about—"

"Yes!" snapped Natalie. "I did make a mistake, okay? A mistake I attempted to rectify. As the Bible says, let he, or in this case *she*, who is without sin be the one to cast the first stone."

"Huh?"

"It's a Bible verse," Kim said quickly. "Kind of a metaphor for not judging others."

"Well, maybe Natalie should pay attention to that one herself," I said. After that, I shut up. And so did Natalie.

"Why do you keep pushing her buttons?" Kim asked me as she and I went into her house. Natalie had already stormed off to her house next door.

"Me?" I gave her an innocent look.

She kind of laughed. "Okay. Nat likes pushing yours too."

I nodded. "Thank you."

"It's probably hard for you to understand, but Nat has this deep need to convert everyone."

"Maybe she should focus more on her own issues."

"Good point. And just so you know, she really has a good heart."

"I'm sure." But as I said this, I could taste the sarcasm on my tongue.

"And if she didn't care about you, she probably wouldn't say half of what she does."

"Wow, I'd hate to hear how she talks to her good friends... like you?"

Kim shrugged. "Trust me, Nat and I have had our own go-rounds for years now. But in the end, when I need someone to stand by me, she's always there."

I wanted to ask why that was a good thing but had a feeling I'd already stepped over the line as well as on some toes.

I'm not going to tell Kim or Natalie that Spencer has been pressuring me to go to the prom with him. He makes these jokes like since I'm new here and he doesn't have a date, we should go. I'm flattered, but there's not the slightest chance I'll go with him. And not because of Natalie's stupid comments. In fact, just hearing her say that makes me want to spend more time with Spencer. Even though I don't want to go to the prom, I might go out with him. Just to show Miss Busybody to mind her own business.

April 29

Something in the house felt odd today. Both Kim and Uncle Allen were very quiet at dinner. As usual, I was ready to fix my own food, but to my surprise Kim urged me to join them. She had even attempted to fix a vegetarian dish of spaghetti and tomato sauce. Of course, it wasn't vegan because it had Parmesan cheese on top, but I didn't scrape it off. And anyway, I've been slacking off a little lately. But mostly I didn't want to offend her, so I actually tried to make some light dinner conversation, but it seemed to go nowhere. Oh, they were polite, but it was like something was wrong. Really wrong. I began to suspect that I had done or said something to offend them. And I quickly finished my food and excused myself, saying that I had homework.

As it turned out, it's the one-year anniversary of my aunt's death. I didn't figure this out until later this evening when I went outside to get some fresh air and to check out the garden. By then the sun was just going down, and it was shadowy and cool, and when I came around a hedge, there was Kim. We both sort of jumped.

"Sorry," I said when I realized I'd startled her. "I didn't know you were out here."

"That's okay."

"Did I do something wrong tonight?" I asked suddenly. "I mean, if I've said something to offend you or maybe Natalie or—"

"No no, not at all…" She held up her hands to stop me. "It's just that I've been thinking about Mom today." Then she explained what day it was.

"Oh, I'm sorry… I guess I forgot… I'm not really good at dates…like birthdays and whatnot." I wanted to add how my own mother often forgot my birthday but didn't see the point.

"That's okay. I wouldn't expect you to remember."

"I wish I had known her..." I looked around the garden. It was really starting to look good. "Being out here in her garden sort of makes me feel like I almost know her."

"You've done some nice things out here." Kim sighed. "I think she'd appreciate that. And I meant to do some weeding and stuff, but I've been so busy with the end of school and getting in scholarship things."

"I don't mind. I love everything about gardening—whether it's weeding or planting or watering or fertilizing. It probably seems weird, but I have always loved getting my hands dirty."

Kim was looking at me now, kind of studying me. "You know what's even weirder, Maya? My mom loved all that too. And it reminds me that you're actually related to her—I mean, even more than I am—when it comes to genetics and DNA. You know what I'm saying?"

I shrugged. "I guess. But you're related to her in a lot more ways than that. According to your dad, you're a lot like her."

She nodded. "Yes. I know."

We stood out there in the dusky light, and Kim told me some of her favorite things about her mom, and by the time she was finished, we were both crying. I know I was crying for her, and her dad, and their loss. But I was also crying for myself. I never had a mother like that. Not ever.

Maya's Green Tip for the Day

Here are a couple of natural gardening tips. (1) One teaspoon each of baking soda and dish soap combined with a gallon of water can protect roses against black spot fungus. (2) Coffee grounds make a good fertilizer. You can sprinkle them around the base of a plant or on the lawn or mix them in your compost.

Nineteen

May 3

Maybe it was because of our talk in the garden, or maybe it was because Natalie was not going, but for whatever reason, I agreed to go with Kim to her youth group meeting tonight. And okay, it was pretty weird sitting in this room with a bunch of Christian kids and trying not to be too rude. Finally I just decided to be myself. It was open discussion time, and the leaders, an attractive couple named Josh and Caitlin Miller, had invited everyone to jump in. Naturally, the Christian kids jumped in. I sat on the sidelines and just observed. And perhaps I spaced out a bit too, because suddenly the focus changed, and Josh Miller was talking to me.

"How about you, Maya?" I could feel the others staring at me now.

"What?" I blinked and sat up straighter.

He smiled, and it was a Brad Pitt sort of dazzling smile. "Sorry to catch you off guard, but I wonder, what question would you ask God if you got the opportunity?"

His wife poked him with her elbow, then laughed. "You'll have to excuse Josh. He can be a little pushy sometimes."

"I'm just curious," he continued. "You don't have to say anything if you don't want to."

"Well…," I began, "if I believed in God, and that is a gigantic *if*, I would ask Him why He lets so many bad things happen. Why do innocent people die in earthquakes or tsunamis? Why do African orphans suffer from AIDS? Why did Hurricane Katrina make so many people homeless?" I almost asked why God lets people like Shannon have children when they obviously don't want them, but I figured I'd thrown enough crud onto the table. Besides that, the room seemed very quiet now, and maybe I had these Christian kids stumped. I wasn't sure whether to be happy or sad.

Josh smiled again. "You remind me of my sister."

Some of the kids kind of chuckled, and I wasn't sure what to think about that. But then Caitlin translated. "You can take that as a huge compliment, Maya. Chloe Miller is an amazing girl. And some of us can remember when she was asking questions a lot like this."

"By the way," added Josh, "that was a really great question."

"But you don't have an answer?" I asked.

"We might not have an answer you'll like," he said. "First of all, God doesn't define 'bad' the same way we do. Sure, He created an earth that's capable of things like earthquakes and tsunamis. God didn't design this planet to go forever. And our earthly lives are a temporary existence. That's why

He created heaven to be an afterlife—something that's made to last through eternity."

Okay, I'm still trying to wrap my head around that one, but I suppose it makes sense to someone with faith.

"I'm not saying God sends earthquakes and catastrophes to kill people," Josh continued. "That's a question that won't get answered until we see God face to face. But I do believe He uses tragedies to remind us that we are mortal. I mean, it might come as a surprise to some people, *but nobody is getting out of this place alive.*"

There were some chuckles at this.

"I'd like to answer part of your question too," Caitlin said. "Some of the sad things you mentioned have more to do with bad choices people make. Take AIDS, for instance. That's a result of people choosing to do things that God has clearly said are wrong. Sometimes people hurt themselves. Sometimes they hurt others. And it doesn't please God at all."

"But God can use these negative things," Kim said. "I've experienced some real pain...and I know how God has used it to teach me things I wouldn't have learned otherwise. Going through the death of my mom has helped me grow into what I hope is a better person."

Some of the others chimed in now too, telling of tough experiences that helped change them, claiming that God used challenging circumstances to make them stronger. Their stories were interesting and genuine, but I suppose it was their enthusiasm that really got my attention. It's like they were excited about their lives.

"Is this making any sense to you?" Caitlin asked me.

I shrugged. "I suppose it all makes perfect sense if you believe in God. But like I said, I'm not convinced."

She just smiled. "Hey, we've all been there."

I frowned. "Really?"

"Oh yeah," Kim said. "You don't think we were born Christians, do you?"

"No...not really." Suddenly I'm remembering Grandma Carolina and things I heard in her church. And as different as this group seems from that congregation of old black people clapping and singing, there is an uncanny similarity. I think it's related to their enthusiasm about life and God. And their hopefulness. I know I don't have that. I doubt I ever will.

"We've all had questions about God," Josh said finally. "And God is not the least bit intimidated by them."

"That's right," said a guy with long dark hair and the clearest blue eyes I've ever seen. "You can throw anything at God—He's a big boy. He can take it."

Then Josh challenged me and everyone else to keep tossing their biggest and hardest questions at God. Josh held up his Bible. "And trust me, this is our best answer book. It's all in here."

"But keep in mind," added Caitlin, "that God won't answer all our questions in this life. There are lots of things He expects us to trust Him for. That's where faith comes in."

They all sort of nodded then, like they totally got this. Although I didn't get it—and I still don't get it. Then Josh said a prayer and led some songs with his guitar. And after that, it was fellowship time, which I figured meant we were supposed to eat junk food (which I passed on) and talk to others (which I wasn't too sure about).

But then the guy with those eyes approached me. "Those were great questions. That's cool that you felt comfortable enough to ask."

I shrugged. "I don't know about that."

He smiled, and I realized he had a great smile too. "Yeah, I guess Josh kind of cornered you. He does that sometimes. But it's a good way to get people to think about what they believe."

"I'm not sure what I believe. And I'm not too sure about God either."

"I hear you." He nodded, then stuck out his hand. "Hey, by the way I'm Dominic Walsh."

"And I'm Maya Stark." We shook hands, and his blue eyes twinkled in a way that reminded me of the Pacific on a sunny day. Okay, I know that sounds totally cornball, but I can't help myself.

"To be honest, I'm not the best one to answer all that many questions. I've only been a Christian for...not even a year yet. And my parents were never churchgoers, so this all still feels pretty new to me. But I do meet with Josh once a week to learn more, and I've been spending a lot of time reading this." He held up what looked like a fairly well-worn Bible.

"I used to have a Bible too," I confessed, not mentioning that it was a small pink one with a zipper. And then for no explainable reason, I told him about my grandmother and her influence, then how she died. "I guess I blamed God...and kind of set the whole religion thing aside."

"Sounds like your grandmother was a cool lady. I'd bet she really cared about you...and still does."

"I don't know..."

"I'm guessing she planted some seeds back then, and she's probably up there in heaven just waiting for them to grow."

Seeds? I knew he meant this as a metaphor. But since I'm a gardener, just the mention of seeds got my attention. That and thinking of my grandma. We talked awhile longer, fortunately moving on to lighter topics, like where I came from and whether or not I liked Harrison High. As we talked, I couldn't help but be drawn to this guy. In fact, he reminded me of Jason—the handsome roadie I fell in love with last winter. But something about Dominic is even more attractive—

and different. I mean, although he's obviously not as old as Jason, it's like he has a maturity beyond his years. And he also has this very straightforward manner, this attitude like he's really at ease with himself and comfortable in his own skin. Well, why shouldn't he be? He's tall and has those gorgeous eyes and that cool smile and great cheekbones. He's really good-looking. Okay, color me shallow...but I'm not blind!

"Hey, if you ever want to talk at school or wherever," he told me as Kim and I were getting ready to leave, "I'm around."

"Thanks. I'll keep that in mind."

And I will keep it in mind. In fact, as I record all this in my journal, it seems to be dominating my mind. Or maybe I'm just using it as a smoke screen to keep from thinking about the other topic of the evening: God. I'm just not sure what I think about that yet.

May 11

I actually went to church with Kim and Uncle Allen today. But only because it was Mother's Day and they were both a little down. Unfortunately, I think all three of us were pretty down by the time the service ended. With the focus on mothers and with all of us feeling deprived in one way or another...well, you'd think preachers would be more understanding!

Uncle Allen invited me to go to lunch with them afterward, but I begged off. I told them I had homework, which was a lie. Although I did want to work on a sketch for art class tomorrow. Mostly I wanted to be alone. But once I got home, I puttered in the garden, which is looking really good. I needed to get out of that house. It's like the walls were closing in on me. So I borrowed Kim's bike, which she had given me permission to do, and I put my sketching stuff in a backpack and took off.

I ended up at this pretty park by the river, found a vacant bench, sat down, and opened my sketchpad and then just sat there like a stone, staring at a blank piece of paper. Finally I forced myself to move the pencil across the page. I decided I would draw the tree near the river, but I barely had the trunk sketched when I couldn't continue. I just stared down at the unfinished tree until it became this blur. And because tears were pouring down my face, it became a soggy blur. So I set it aside.

Okay, I knew I was doing some sort of grieving. And as weird as it seems, I knew I was partly grieving the loss of my own mother. Oh, Shannon's not dead. But she's been convicted and moved to the state penitentiary. She's doing time. My dad called me Thursday night to inform me that she had been sentenced to five years for possessing and delivering a controlled substance—cocaine.

"Delivering?" I asked.

"Yes. Apparently she was involved in some sleazy business venture to make some fast money."

I'm sure I swore when I heard this. And Dad acted like he hadn't heard me. I'm also sure Lynnette had as much to do with this as Shannon. Not that it matters. My mom is a fool.

"Shannon could've been sentenced for as much as twenty years," he told me, like that was supposed to make me feel better. "And according to her attorney, she's going to appeal her sentence anyway."

"Does she have much of a chance?"

"I doubt it." He sighed loudly. "I feel really bad about this, Maya. I feel like you were dealt a pretty sad hand when it came to parents."

For his sake I tried to brighten up a bit. "Hey, it's not your fault that Shannon's a mess. At least she had a decent sister."

He kind of laughed. "Yeah, there's something to be thankful for."

We talked a little longer, but I could tell he had other things to do. Like getting some sleep since it was the middle of the night in Paris. But before he hung up, he gave me the address of the prison. "Shannon would love to hear from you."

I told him that I'd write her. But even as I said it, I knew it was a lie. Why should I write her? Why should I care if she rots in prison? And yet as I sat there on that park bench, all I could think was that my mom was locked up, probably wearing one of those ugly orange jumpsuits, probably completely depressed—on Mother's Day. Sure, it was her own stupid fault that she was in there, but how could I not feel sorry for her?

So I picked up my pencil, and although the paper was still soggy, I wrote over the unfinished trunk of the tree, "Happy Mother's Day, Shannon. I'm sure you've seen better days. Take care. Maya." Then I folded it and stuffed it into my backpack. I may send it. Or I may not. I doubt that a note like that would bring her much comfort. Mostly I don't care. I don't want to think about her. I can't.

Maya's Green Tip for the Day

I wonder if a prison could be considered a human recycling center. You turn in your messed-up, dirty, rotten scoundrel and pick her up later, all shiny and clean and new. No, I don't think so. And I don't think I have a green tip for the day either.

Twenty

May 23

I've kept pretty much to myself these past couple of weeks. I haven't gotten into any big arguments with Natalie about anything. I don't even open my mouth. I know Kim thinks I'm depressed, and she's tried to encourage me with some little pep talks and even suggested counseling. I pretend to listen to her, but I think I'm permanently tuned out. Apparently her dad told her about Shannon's sentencing, because the two of them have been treating me like an explosive device, like they don't want to set me off. Whatever.

And I haven't really talked to anyone at school either. Not even Dominic, who always waves and smiles. I'm sure Marissa and Jake think I have a serious personality disorder. Or that I'm a witch or a zombie girl since I won't even sit with them at lunch anymore. I've been packing my own lunch and eating outside. And maybe they're right—maybe I am disturbed. Or maybe I'm simply depressed. Maybe I do need some kind of therapy. Or maybe I just need time.

Most of my focus has been on school and getting everything ready for my emancipation, which looks like it can happen this summer. Also, I've been getting in my driving time. Uncle Allen has been very accommodating. And he doesn't even seem to mind that I don't want to talk. He actually takes along a book or a crossword puzzle to work on as I drive around like a mute girl and slowly log in my hours. I'm up to almost thirty now. And some are at night.

May 24

I feel like I'm seriously losing it tonight. Like I may be cracking up. That, like my mom, I may need to be locked up. Oh, I haven't broken any laws. But I cannot stop crying. No one is home tonight. Uncle Allen is playing poker with his buddies from the newspaper where he works. I'm sure he was relieved to get away from me. I feel bad that I am contaminating their home with my gloom. And Kim begged me to go to youth group with her tonight, but I put on my blank face and declined.

Since they left, I have done nothing but cry...well, that and consider the easiest way to end this pain. I mean, really, what is the point? As I mentioned when I started this journal of craziness, (1) life is not fair, and (2) it's not going to get any better. Really, why should it? How can it?

But one thing is clear. If I were to end my life—which is a distinct possibility—I would not do it here. Not in this house that has already suffered a severe loss just a little over a year ago. No, I couldn't do that to Kim and Uncle Allen. I couldn't do that to my deceased aunt Patricia either.

I've been thinking about my aunt a lot tonight. I've wandered around the house and wished that her ghost would appear to me and tell me something—anything that could make sense of this madness that is called my life. But she hasn't shown up. Then I began thinking of Grandma Carolina. But I know what she would tell me—the same things she told me when I was a little girl. "You just lean on God, baby girl. He'll never let you down. Just hold on tight to His hand, and He'll take care of you. He always does."

But I don't believe that anymore. For one thing, God has let me down. Again and again and again and again. And yet...there is this small part of me that's not sure. Maybe I'm the one who let Him down. Maybe I'm the one who let go of His hand.

May 25

I pretended to sleep in this morning. I knew that if I were up and around, Kim would ask me to go to church with her and her dad. But I didn't want to go. Yet as soon as they were gone, I started to cry again. Really, I don't know how long I can go on like this. What is wrong with me?

Later that same day...

"I want to talk to you," Kim told me in a serious voice. She found me sitting out in the garden...rather, hiding in the garden. Or so I thought. I was sitting on an upside-down bucket behind a section of raspberries that her mother must've planted years ago.

"Is something wrong?" I asked as I stood up.

"Yes."

So, worried that something might be wrong with her dad, I followed her over to the picnic table, and we sat across from each other. "What is it?" I asked.

"It's you."

I let out a sigh and tried not to roll my eyes.

"You're depressed, Maya."

Okay, then I rolled my eyes. "Ya think?"

She actually smiled then. "Yes. And I think you need help."

"Help?"

"Like I said before, you need counseling or something."

I just shrugged.

"And I talked to Caitlin Miller about—"

I quickly stood up. "You're talking to other people about me?" I said, towering over her. "Behind my back?"

"It's not like that. I only asked—"

"Look, Kim, I may have problems, but they are *my* problems, okay?" I glared down at her. "And I'm sorry if my problems are putting a damper on your perfect little life. I'm sure you'll be so glad when I'm not living here anymore, and I'm working on it. Okay? I plan to be out of here by the end of June. Will that be—"

"That's not it, Maya." She was standing now too. "It's just that I'm worried about you."

"Well, don't be."

"You're so unhappy, and I know why."

I narrowed my eyes at her. "You know why, do you?"

"Yes. You really do need God in your—"

"You sound just like your stupid best friend now!"

"Natalie might not have the best approach, but she's right about that, Maya. You do need God, and you'll never be happy until you figure that out."

"I'm glad you know so much about me, Kim. I'm glad you know what I need. I suppose it hasn't occurred to you that I've had one seriously messed-up life. That I have a mom doing time for drugs. That I have a dad who doesn't give a—"

"We all have something difficult to deal with, Maya. You know that. But without God, we crumble. And that's what you're doing right now. You are crumbling...and you can't even see it."

I took in a deep breath then, ready to throw some more mean words at her, but it was like they were stuck. So I just turned and stomped into the house, went to my room, and quietly shut the door. But I knew that she had nailed it. I am crumbling. I feel like I'm being smashed and pulverized into this sad little heap of...misery.

So I did something I thought I would never do. I got down on my knees, and I began to pray. Not the way I used to pray with my grandma, those sweet little prayers before bedtime. And probably not the way most people pray. But I began to just dump it all out. Like I was pouring out all the crud and mess and the stinking garbage of my life—piling it in front of God (if He was even listening)—and not caring how rotten or hopeless it all sounded. I didn't even care if I was insulting Him. Hadn't someone in Kim's youth group said that you couldn't hurt God's feelings? Well, I was determined to give it my best shot. If He wanted to strike me dead with a lightning bolt, I was like—*bring it!*

But He didn't bring it. In fact, a very strange thing happened when I was finally done. As I was sitting on the edge of the bed, blowing my nose and wiping my eyes, I realized that I had this weird feeling, this almost unrecognizable sensation. So unfamiliar I had to ask myself what it was.

It was *peace.* I felt a sensation of peace inside me. A quiet calmness that was so tangible, so real...I suddenly became fearful that it might go away. So I decided to take a walk. Don't ask me why. It just seemed like a good idea. Perhaps taking a walk would somehow seal in this peace. And as I walked, I knew that the peace must've come from God.

But I wasn't even sure why. Or how. Or if it would stay with me. All I knew was that I wanted it to stay with me.

Then before I went to bed, I knocked on Kim's door. She looked surprised to see me but invited me to come in. She had been working on something on her computer. Something she obviously didn't want me to see since she'd just turned off the screen, although I could still hear it humming.

"I just wanted to say I'm sorry," I began.

"I'm sorry too. I probably came on too strong and—"

"No...you were right."

"I was right?"

"Yes. When you said I was crumbling...well, you pretty much nailed it. I have been crumbling."

"Oh..."

"Anyway, I don't exactly know what it means, but I actually prayed today. It's the first time I've prayed in a long, long time."

She smiled now. "Cool."

"I guess. I mean, all I know is I prayed and sort of dumped a lot of stuff on God. And then I got this really amazing sense of peace." I looked curiously at her now, wondering if she would get it.

She nodded. "Oh yeah. I know exactly what you mean."

"Really?"

"It's a supernatural kind of peace, right?"

"Yeah. I mean, I could really feel it."

She nodded again. "It's from God, Maya."

"I guess I knew that." I took a deep breath. "Anyway, I was also thinking about what you were saying about Caitlin and the counseling thing...and I think I'd like to meet with her."

"She's not a certified counselor, but she's really good at listening. And then if you need someone with more training, you know, for anything serious, she could recommend some good resources." Kim wrote down a phone number and handed it to me. "Just give her a call."

"Thanks."

And so I'm thinking maybe I will. I'm not sure that it will do any good, but I guess it couldn't hurt.

May 27

I met with Caitlin after school today. I would've canceled it, except I had already arranged for her to pick me up, and I didn't want to be rude. The reason I wanted to cancel was probably just a case of cold feet. I wasn't sure that I really wanted to take the next step in whatever this is. Also, my week so far has been going pretty well. I mean, I've been talking to people again, and I am starting to feel sort of okay.

I suppose the main reason I didn't cancel with Caitlin was because I was worried about what would happen if I didn't talk to someone. What if this feeling of peace went away? And already, it seemed to be fading slightly. And that scared me.

Caitlin took me to a coffee shop called the Paradiso, and after a little encouragement, I told her what was going on with me. Instead of going into all the details of my past (although I did tell her that my mom was doing time), I mostly described what happened to me Sunday afternoon...and how it felt authentic and beyond me but that I didn't know how to hold on to it. I didn't understand it. Maybe I needed help. "But it felt really real—like maybe it could change my life," I said finally.

She set down her cup and smiled. "That was definitely God."

I slowly nodded. "I kind of thought so too. But I'm just not sure what I'm supposed to do with it."

"Did you invite God into your heart, Maya?"

Naturally, this took me by surprise. Besides being a fairly personal question, it was kind of confusing. "I'm not sure. I mean, a long time ago when I was eleven and I went forward in my grandmother's church, I prayed with the preacher and invited Jesus into my heart." I peered at Caitlin. "So what's the difference between God and Jesus anyway? In my grandmother's church it was always 'Jesus this' and 'Jesus that.'" To be honest, I'm not sure if I was just trying to distract her with this question or if I really wanted to know.

"I think of God and Jesus as one. I mean, God, in the role of the Father, did send Jesus to earth in the form of man so

He could die on the cross...and that's how we get forgiveness. I assume you've heard all that before?"

"I've heard it. And when I was a kid, it sort of made sense. But after my grandmother died, well, nothing made sense."

"I think you need to invite Jesus into your heart again, Maya. Just so you can be sure."

I took a deep breath, worried that she expected me to do this thing right there in the coffee shop. "I'll think about it."

"He's knocking on the door of your heart," she continued. "And I think when you prayed to Him on Sunday, you cracked that door open just a little. And that's how His peace slipped in. And naturally it was a huge comfort. I think He was giving you a sample of what's in store."

"So if I do this, if I ask God into my heart again, you're saying that peace will continue?"

"Oh, we all have trials and doubts and times when it feels like God has turned His back on us. But for the most part, that peace sticks around. Well, unless we turn our backs on God. Then I think He takes the peace away. Not to be mean, of course, but just to remind us that we need to return to Him to get it back. Does that make sense?"

"Maybe..."

The truth is, it makes perfect sense. I was the one who had turned my back on God. I walked away from Him because I felt He'd let me down. I wonder how things might've gone differently if I hadn't. And yet it's too mind-boggling to go there. All I can deal with at the moment is *now*.

Anyway, Caitlin and I talked some more. She asked me some specific questions about my past as well as my plans for the future, and I tried to be honest. I think she was trying to determine if I needed some serious psychological care or not. But she didn't make any recommendations. Although she did ask if I'd like to meet with her on a weekly basis.

"Why?" I asked, knowing that probably sounded rude.

But she just laughed. "Because I care about you, Maya. And I meet with some other girls. I used to meet with your cousin. I think it all started back when I was in high school and began meeting with Chloe." Suddenly her eyes lit up. "Well, speak of the devil." Then she winked at me. "She's really an angel." She waved to a dark-haired girl who was just coming into the coffee shop. The next thing I knew, Caitlin was introducing me to Chloe, explaining that I was Kim's cousin.

"Chloe is not only my favorite sister-in-law—"

"You mean your *only* sister-in-law," teased Chloe.

"But she's also a rock star." Caitlin beamed at her. "Did you guys just get back from tour?"

"Just in time for graduation." Chloe fiddled with a silver stud that pierced her eyebrow. Now I'm not opposed to body piercing on other people, but it's not really my thing.

"Oh, you're *that* Chloe," I said as I put together that this was the musician person Marissa and Spencer had talked about. "I've heard a lot about you."

"Yeah, I've got quite the reputation," Chloe said.

"She's our local celebrity," Caitlin said, "along with her band."

"And you're Kim Peterson's cousin?" Chloe said with a curious expression.

"Yeah, can't you see the family resemblance?" I joked. She laughed.

"Are you guys going to play the Paradiso while you're home?" asked Caitlin. Then the two of them explained how this was the very coffeehouse where Chloe got her first break as a musician.

"I was so scared that day," Chloe said. And then they started talking about all that had happened since then and how the latest leg of the tour had gone. I was half listening and half thinking about what Caitlin had told me about asking God into my heart.

"Sorry, Maya," Chloe said suddenly. "You must be bored with all this music biz."

"No, not at all." Then I lowered my voice. "In fact, it's pretty familiar territory... My dad's a musician too."

"Really?" Chloe leaned forward, her brows lifted with interest. "Anyone we'd know?"

"Well, most people our age haven't heard of him. And

I don't really like talking about it, but his name is Nick Stark, and he was—"

"Nick Stark is your dad?" Chloe looked at Caitlin with wide eyes. "My mom is going to have a fit."

"She's a huge Nick Stark fan," admitted Caitlin. "She actually wanted Josh and me to use one of his songs for our wedding."

"But they didn't," added Chloe.

"No offense," Caitlin said.

I laughed. "None taken. I doubt that I'd use one of my dad's songs at my own wedding." Then we all laughed.

"Well, I just came in to say hey and grab a mocha." Chloe smiled at me. "Very cool to meet you, Maya Stark." She turned to Caitlin now. "Hey, why don't you invite us all for dinner so Mom can meet Nick Stark's daughter?"

Caitlin looked at me. "Would you be willing? I mean, I understand you wanting your anonymity and everything."

"Oh, come on," urged Chloe. "I live with this stuff every day."

"Sure," I told them both. "Why not?"

After Chloe left, Caitlin reminded me of my promise to think about inviting God into my heart. "I'll probably bug you about it now," she said. "Just to see where you are with it. But don't worry, I know it's kind of a timing thing too. Just don't put it off for too long."

I told her I wouldn't. And as it turned out, I was telling her the truth.

Shortly after Caitlin dropped me off at home, I went into my room and got down on my knees, and I asked Jesus to come into my heart. I wasn't quite sure how to put the words, but I tried to do it the same way I had done it when I was eleven. And it wasn't even that hard, because it was a prayer I'd heard the preacher say almost every single Sunday that I went to church with my grandma. Okay, I'm sure I might've missed something, but I think I got the gist of it. I asked Jesus back into my heart, and I asked Him to forgive me, and then I said, "Amen." And when I was finished, it felt like it "took." And the peace was back—stronger than ever.

Still, I'm not quite sure I want to tell anyone. Not just yet anyway. In case I was wrong and it didn't take. I suppose that doesn't sound very faithful, but it's the truth.

May 31

I went with Uncle Allen to Kim's graduation tonight. She was pretty nervous about the whole thing, which seemed silly to me. I mean, it was just a graduation. You walk across the stage, and the principal hands you a diploma. It couldn't be as hard as modeling. But I had no idea that my cousin was the valedictorian. Wow. I was really impressed. Not just by the fact that she'd maintained a perfect GPA, but by her speech. It was so cool.

Of course, as I sat there with Uncle Allen, I felt a whole crazy, mixed-up mess of emotions. I mean, I really had to admire Kim and what she'd accomplished. But at the same time, I felt seriously jealous. I knew I would never be able to do anything like that. Because when I considered how she'd been raised…her loving, supportive parents…and how vastly different it was from how I'd been raised, I got kind of mad about the unfairness of it all. But that was stupid. I felt proud that Kim was my cousin. Yet I felt sad that I wasn't going to be part of this family after I got emancipated this summer and moved out. And at the same time I thought I should be thankful that I had gotten to live with them at all.

On top of everything else, as Kim talked about her friends and school and fun memories, I began to question myself—whether I might need to keep going to high school too.

I'd recently been thinking that with my GED and emancipation, I might get an apartment and a job and start taking college classes next year. Mrs. King told me that was a real possibility if my SAT scores were as high as she expected them to be. But suddenly I'm not sure I really want that. Part of me wants to be like Kim, with friends like she has, just going to high school and living my life. Anyway, the whole time I was sitting there for Kim's graduation, I felt like I was stuck in this weird emotional Ping-Pong game. Back and forth, back and forth. Even now I'm confused.

June 7

I went to youth group with Kim tonight. And when it was sharing time, I stood up and made a "public confession." I'd already told Caitlin when we met for the second time just yesterday. Then I told Kim on our way to youth group. But I decided it was time to let my little cat out of the bag in a big way. So I announced to everyone in the room that I'd invited God into my heart and that from now on I wanted to live my life for Him.

"Okay," I admitted, "I don't know what that means exactly. But I'm sure I'll find out over time."

They all clapped and congratulated me. And during the fellowship time, Dominic came over and gave me a big hug. That was pretty cool.

"And the thing is," Josh said as he shook my hand, "you don't walk your faith alone, Maya. It's like you're part of this great big, happy family now."

"Yes," Caitlin said. "Although sometimes we can be a slightly dysfunctional family too. But that's part of the fun, right?"

"That's right," Kim said. "We have to learn to get along and forgive each other and all kinds of good stuff."

And so, for the first time in a long time, I feel like I'm really part of a family again. And okay, I'm not stupid. I realize that some of these people might let me down from time to time. I mean, they are only human. But at the same time, I realize that with God as my Father...well, I think I can make it.

Ironically, I have filled up this whole journal, and when I reread the first sentence of my first entry (written more than a year ago), I had to laugh. Because I was wrong. Totally wrong. For starters, I thought life was unfair. And okay, it can seem unfair—but that's without God. I think that God must somehow even things out. Or at least that's what I'm hoping. And that brings me to the second thing—I was so hopeless and certain that things were only going to get worse. And yes, they did get worse for me. But again that was *without* God. With God, I am feeling confident that things are only going to get better.

Do I have all the answers now? Like where will I live next year? Or will I still get my emancipation? Or will I continue going to Harrison High? I can't really say right now. But I do believe that God has the answers. And I do believe that not only is He going to show me, but He's going to walk with me—every step of the way. And it's going to be good!

Maya's Green Tip for the Day

Here's a thought. Maybe we all need to consider who
created the earth. And if that's God, which I have finally
come to believe, then maybe we need to ask Him what
He'd like us to do to take better care of it. For me, I
think I should start taking better care of my own heart
first. Then maybe I'll get some more practical ideas for
the planet later.

1. Maya started out this book feeling lost and hopeless. Have you ever felt like that? Describe what made you feel that way and how you handled it.

2. Were you surprised to learn that Maya was vegan? Why do you think she made this decision?

3. Why do you think Maya felt so compromised when she started working in the fashion industry? Have you ever felt compromised like that? Explain.

4. Maya's relationship with Shannon wasn't exactly typical. How is it similar to or different from your relationship with your mother or guardian?

5. If you could've talked to Shannon, what would you have told her?

6. Maya seemed to accept her dad's commitment to his career. How did you feel about it? What would you have told him?

7. What did you think about Maya's emancipation plan? Do you think it was right? wrong? Why?

8. Were you surprised that Shannon returned to using drugs? Why or why not?

9. What do you think Maya's relationship with Shannon should be like now that Shannon is in prison?

10. Maya has a big decision to make about whether to live on her own and go to college or to continue high school. What would you advise her to do?

11. How did you feel when Maya finally committed her life to God? Have you made a similar commitment? Describe how your life has changed since then.

The Secret Life of Samantha McGregor series

A powerful gift requires a lot of responsibility...

Bad Connection

Kayla Henderson is missing, and everyone, including Samantha, assumes she ran away. But then Samantha has a vision. If Kayla really is in danger, then time is running out!

Beyond Reach

Garrett Pierson is one of those quiet, academic types. One day, Samantha has a vision of Garrett teetering on a railroad bridge - and then falling backwards, just beyond reach! What does this vision mean, and...where is Garrett, anyway?

Playing with Fire

Samantha's brother, Zach, is finally home after rehab for his meth addiction. Then Sam has a vision of a burning cabin, and a shooting. Convinced that Zach is involved somehow, Sam must decide whether to risk getting Zach in trouble with the law - or ultimately risk his life.

Payback

Samantha is plunged into her biggest challenges yet, as she works against the clock to stop a mass murder, help a troubled youth, and save her mother from making a terrible mistake!

Diary of a Teenage Girl series
Meet Caitlin, Chloe, and Kim

Experience the lives of three very different girls, Caitlin, Chloe, and Kim through the pages of their diaries. Caitlin, the conservative Christian struggles to stand morally strong and pure; Chloe, the alternative rocker wants to be authentic to who she is and follow Christ; and Kim, adopted from a Korean orphanage as a baby, searches out her true identity. Despite their unique perspectives on all life throws at them, they join together in their pursuit of a closer relationship with God.

www.doatg.com